'The story is teasing and suspenseful, and written
with vivacity and elegance.'
Sunday Times, Book of the Week

'Tania Unsworth writes beautifully, and it's hard
not to get caught in the current of this magical tale
about family and identity.' *The Times*

'Lyrical writing with a hint of dark magic in a tale of
grief, loss and finding yourself.' *The Bookseller*

'Another triumph from the dark pen
of Tania Unsworth. A master at combining reality
with tinges of dark fantasy, and beguiling the reader
with intrigues of what is real and what is
make-believe.' *Minerva Reads*

'This is a perfectly told story which twists fantasy
into reality in an oh-so satisfying way. Tania
Unsworth draws in the reader with her beautiful
writing and intensity of plot – an intensity that
nevertheless still feels perfectly paced.'
That Boy Can Teach

'Written in flowing prose, this might not be a traditional mermaid tale, set under the sea, but it is a well-crafted, lyrical story of family relationships and self-discovery with a touch of fantasy.'
The School Librarian

'With a highly original concept, mesmerising storytelling, a beautifully portrayed exploration of character, identity and relationships, I highly recommend this for Years 5-6.'
Books for Topics

'Beautiful descriptions weave their way through, bringing the characters, plot and landscapes to life.'
Mr Davies' Reads

'I finished it with a happy-sad smile, happy that it had been such a pleasurable read, and sad that it was over. This is definitely one I'd recommend.'
The Bookbag

'The realistic and the magical are intertwined with exquisite skill... This story is a rare treat, being powerfully and beautifully memorable.'
Carousel

The Girl who thought her Mother was a Mermaid

Tania Unsworth spent her childhood in Cambridge before moving to America in her early twenties. She comes from a family of writers and lives in Boston, USA, with her husband and two sons.

Tania Unsworth

The Girl who thought her Mother was a Mermaid

ZEPHYR

First published in the UK in 2018 by Zephyr,
an imprint of Head of Zeus Ltd
This paperback edition first published in 2019
by Head of Zeus Ltd

Text copyright © Tania Unsworth, 2018
Art copyright © Helen Crawford-White, 2018

9 7 5 3 1 2 4 6 8

A catalogue record for this book is available
from the British Library.

ISBN (PB): 9781788541688
ISBN (E): 9781788541664

Typeset and designed by Lindsay Nash

Printed and bound in Great Britain by
CPI Group (UK) Ltd, Croydon, CR0 4YY

Head of Zeus Ltd
First Floor East
5–8 Hardwick Street
London EC1R 4RG

WWW.HEADOFZEUS.COM

For my mother,
who also came from far away

One

The first time Stella Martin ran away, it was in her sleep. The second was by accident. But the third time she did it on purpose, to find out whether she was human or not.

The sleepwalking began when she was eight, soon after her mum died, and at first Stella didn't get any further than her bedroom door. The moment she touched the handle — which had always been slightly loose — it rattled and woke her. One night, though, the door was left ajar and there was nothing to stop her passing through, into the silent, carpeted corridor beyond.

She padded down the broad staircase, across the hall, into the kitchen where the marble countertops, polished by Mrs Chapman every day, gleamed liquid in the moonlight. Out of the back door she went, on to the patio, moving without hesitation, as if on command.

The grass was wet from the sprinklers, but Stella didn't seem to notice the chill on her bare toes. She stepped on to the lawn, still fast asleep, passing through the circle of light from the porch lantern, moving into deeper and deeper shadow. When she reached the low stone wall, she swung her legs over, her feet finding the flagstones on the other side.

Ten metres away lay the swimming pool, its water black as flint.

It was lucky Stella's dad was having another of his sleepless nights. Luckier still that, sunk in his trance of sorrow, he had forgotten to lower the window, and happened to catch sight of Stella's fluttering white nightgown. Even so, he was almost too late. Stella's body was tilting towards the water when he caught her around the waist and pulled her to safety.

Stella's mum had loved the pool. She had been a superb swimmer. It wasn't just that she was fast, there was more to it than that. It was the way she used to move. As if she was made of water itself.

She had taught Stella how to swim. Stella could remember the feel of her mum's hand cupping the back of her head. Her mum's smiling face blocked out the sun, and her hair glittered at the edges like a red-gold crown.

I've got you, she had said, as Stella hesitated. *I've got you*.

Stella raised her body and suddenly she was floating. Her fear had gone. For a moment, staring wide-eyed at the sky, she felt as if it would never come back. Her mum had taken it away; the fear Stella had, and all she would ever have, even if she lived to be a hundred years old.

But after the sleepwalking incident, Stella didn't want to go swimming. The sight of the pool frightened her, and she was glad when her dad finally had it emptied and covered with a heavy tarp.

'Such a waste,' Mrs Chapman said, casting a disapproving look at the dead leaves on the surface of the tarp. 'And all because of a little sleepwalking! Do you recall what you were dreaming about?'

Stella nodded. She had been dreaming she was in the pool. It was daytime. Reflections danced against the white walls and bottom of the pool, holding the water in a shimmering net of light. The net would hold her too, she thought, as she waded further in. But a cloud passed over the sun and the net vanished, and there was suddenly nothing beneath her reaching feet. The bottom of the pool had disappeared and she was sinking, deeper and deeper. She twisted her head and looked up. The surface of the water was already far away, the light dwindling. Below her desperately kicking feet she sensed nothing but a vast emptiness. She was descending fast, unable to stop or cry for help, down, down, to a place so deep and dark that she could never come back...

Stella opened her mouth to explain all this to Mrs Chapman, and then closed it again.

'Well?' Mrs Chapman prompted. 'What was it?'

Stella didn't know how to describe the feeling of the dream, the panic. 'It's a secret,' she said finally.

Mrs Chapman ruffled Stella's messy hair. 'What a strange girl you are!'

Stella didn't argue. Mrs Chapman ran the house. She cooked their meals, and kept the floors spotless, and knew where everything was. And if Mrs Chapman said she was strange, it was probably true. Stella was filled with a mysterious dread.

It was exactly the same as the terrible, sinking feeling in her dream.

Two

Stella lived in a part of the country where the towns looked exactly the same as each other, and the land was perfectly flat. The light was flat too, with nothing but the occasional water tower to cast a shadow. The wind blew dust along the ground, clouds crossed the sky, and cars travelled the long, straight roads, without leaving a mark. The land stayed unchanged. As if the wind and the clouds and the cars had never passed by at all.

It was the same with Stella's mum after she died. Her things were put in boxes, and one day even the boxes disappeared. It felt almost as if she had never lived there.

But not quite. On the living room windowsill —
right in the corner — Stella's mum had once made a
pencil sketch of a lamppost. You could see the real
lamppost through the window, on the street beyond
the house. Stella sometimes stood there, looking from
the real lamppost to the drawing and back again, as
if she could somehow get inside her mum's head even
though she wasn't there any longer.

Her mum had often drawn things, although hardly
ever in her notebook. Instead she used whatever
happened to be around; an old receipt, the flap on
a cereal box, a corner of a newspaper. For a while
after she had gone, Stella kept finding the drawings
in unexpected places. A sketch of a tree in the back
of a book. A tiny elephant on a shopping list lying in
the kitchen cabinet.

The cabinet was a jumble of mugs and jugs and
wine glasses because Stella's mum had always stored
everything together. It was the same in her small
vegetable garden, where radishes sprouted among the
carrots, and the herbs and lettuces were all mixed up.
It was as if she didn't notice — or see the need of — rows
and borders, and separate places for things.

One year, for Stella's birthday, her mum had hung

fairy lights under the dining room table, and the three of them had eaten supper sitting on the rug, the edges of the tablecloth hanging down like the walls of a glowing tent.

But after her mum died, Mrs Chapman came to be their housekeeper. The mugs in the kitchen were made to line up, and the vegetable garden returned to lawn, and every meal was served where it ought to be. Stella didn't find any more of her mum's drawings, although she continued to look for them, more out of habit than any real hope. Despite her efforts, her memories began to grow thin.

She began to wonder whether she was remembering her real mum, or just the photo by her bed.

She would have liked to ask her dad, but talking about Stella's mum made his face change, and his voice falter. For a long time after she died, he didn't talk much about anything. He ran a large company and had to travel a lot for work. He was often away from home for days and days.

Whenever she was feeling particularly lonely, Stella would go and look at the picture of the sea. When her mum was alive, the painting had hung in the dining room. Now it was kept in a spare room at the back of the house. Stella didn't know who had painted it, or where it had come from, but she felt sure her mum had liked it.

In her memories, her mum had always been smiling, or laughing. But sometimes another expression would cross her face. It wasn't sadness, or even thoughtfulness, it was much too still for that. As if her mind was so far away that her body had simply been left behind.

That expression had often been on her mum's face when she looked at the painting of the sea.

It was an unusual picture. First, because it was extremely big, almost taking up the whole wall and, second, because despite its size, there was hardly anything in it. There was no white-sailed yacht tacking against the wind, or fishing boat struggling home in stormy seas, or lonely lighthouse, or anything you normally found in pictures of the sea. There was just sky and choppy water, rising in weighty peaks and deep green troughs all the way to the horizon.

Stella sat in the spare room and stared at the picture. There was something mesmerising about its emptiness. If she looked at it long enough, the walls of the room seemed to fall away, and the painted sea looked more and more real, until she felt she was actually there.

Her hand moved up to touch the stone that hung around her neck from a gold chain. It had been a gift from her mum, and Stella had never taken it off from the moment it was given to her.

At first glance, the stone looked like an ordinary pebble. But it was marbled with fine green veins, and when it caught the light in the right way, it gleamed with a dark fire, richer than velvet. The day Stella had been given it was the last time she had ever seen her mum.

It was in the hospital. Her mum was in bed, under a long strip of cold light. Her hair was spread out, covering the whole pillow, and it shone like polished copper. It looked even more beautiful than usual against the white bed linen in that bare, white room.

When she saw Stella, her mum's hand crept from under the covers. The necklace lay in her palm.

'It's the best thing I have,' her mum said.

'What is it?'

Stella could hear the ticking of the clock on the wall above the bed.

'Keep it safe,' her mum said. At least Stella *thought* that was what she said.

She took the necklace. The stone was still warm.

'What is it?' she asked again.

Her mum's hand was a small, empty cup on top of the sheet. 'It's the word of the sea,' she said, her voice faint.

Stella didn't understand. She wanted to push the necklace back into her mum's hand and tell her that she couldn't possibly give it away, because when she got better, she would wear it herself.

Stella stood helplessly by her side.

'Mum?' she whispered.

She climbed on to the bed and laid her head on the still form beneath the sheets, her ear pressed to her mum's heart. As if she was listening at the mouth of some rare, fragile shell, hoping to hear the ocean inside. Yet no sound came.

Three

When Stella was nearly ten, she started a new school and she became aware of something for the first time in her life: there were rules to making friends.

Perhaps the rules were new, like the school, or perhaps they had always been there without her knowing. It didn't really matter either way, because she still didn't have the slightest idea how they worked.

She stood in the middle of the playground, and kids jostled and raced around her as if she was invisible.

After school, she sat at the dining table at home and played drafts with her dad. He used to be good at playing games but since her mum died, he had forgotten how to. He spent a long time staring at the board, and Stella often had to remind him when it was his turn.

'Now I've got you!' he said after each move, his voice bright, as if he was having the time of his life. '*Now*, I've got you!'

'I guess you have,' Stella said, letting him win for the third time in a row.

'Why don't we ever go on holiday to the seaside?' she asked, out of the blue.

'Well,' he said, 'it's a long way away. I think we live about as far from the sea as anyone can.'

'Mum always said "maybe next year", but we never did.'

Stella wanted to ask him why. If her mum had liked the painting of the sea, wouldn't she have liked the real thing even more? But she was silenced by the look of sadness that instantly spread over his face.

'No,' he said. 'No, we never did...'

Outside, rain drummed flatly on the tarp covering the swimming pool.

'Another game?' he said, trying valiantly to smile.

She shook her head.

'How about Snakes and Ladders, then? That's always fun.'

Snakes and Ladders *was* fun – for six year olds, Stella thought.

'It's okay,' she said. 'I'm kind of tired.'

With her dad away so much, and Mrs Chapman busy around the house, Stella needed someone to look after her. Her first nanny couldn't speak English very well, and spent most of her time writing long, tear-stained letters home.

Stella's second nanny never *stopped* talking. Her name was Deb, and it was her chattering that was to blame on the day that Stella ran away by accident. At least, that's what Mrs Chapman said, although Stella knew the whole thing had really been her fault.

It happened after she started at the new school, when her class was taken to the Natural History Museum for the day. Deb got chatting with a couple of the other helpers on the coach, and by the time they arrived at the museum, she was deep in conversation.

Stella's class was studying rocks, and the museum had a room full of them. There were geodes and quartz, and pillars of crystal a metre high, sparkling in a hundred different colours. A man who worked at the museum explained that the rocks didn't look like that when they were in the earth. They had been sliced and polished to reveal their true colours.

Stella felt sorry for them, cut open and forced to give up their secrets.

The man was bald, and his bare head shone. Perhaps he polished it along with the rocks, Stella thought, her mind wandering. He handed out pieces of paper and everybody split up to collect information about the exhibits.

Stella stood before a lump of jagged silver pyrite. If she squinted, it looked a bit like a castle. There were the towers, the outline of the battlements. She squinted harder and a door appeared, although it was more like a cave than a door. Perhaps it was an abandoned castle, falling into ruin, probably haunted...

She looked down at her piece of paper. She hadn't written anything. Any moment, one of the teachers would notice, and tell her to pay attention. They often told her that.

Stella has a tendency to drift, a teacher had once written on her report, and the word 'drift' had been underlined twice.

'Excuse me?'

Stella gave a guilty start. It was the man with the polished head.

'I couldn't help noticing your necklace,' he said. 'I wonder if I could have a look at it.'

Stella's hand instantly shot to her neck.

'It's most unusual, I don't think I've ever seen a stone quite like it before,' the man said. His eyes glittered.

'My mum gave it to me.'

'I'd like, if you don't mind, to examine it.'

Stella shook her head. What if he sliced and polished it, and put it in one of his glass cases? Her mum had told her to keep it safe.

'Just for a moment?' His voice was wheedling. Stella looked for Deb, but she was sitting on the far side of the hall, still chatting.

Stella didn't know what to do.

'I have to use the bathroom!' She turned and ran out of the hall, into the corridor.

She had seen a bathroom earlier in the day; it had been fairly near the main entrance. She went left at the end of the corridor, then right, then left again when it became clear she was heading in the wrong direction.

Stella's panic deepened. Then she turned a corner and saw another hall, and her fear was suddenly forgotten.

The Gallery of Ocean Life read a sign above the entrance. It was a vast space, flooded with sunlight. Glass cases lined the walls. From the high, arched ceiling hung life-sized models of dolphins, sharks and manta rays, although what immediately drew her eye was a massive skeleton of a whale, suspended right in the centre.

Stella stepped forward softly, gazing upward. The whale looked as if it was flying. Its vast jaw, its cavern of ribs, its spine like a great highway stretching to the far horizon. Stella tried to picture how the animal looked when it was alive, with flesh covering its bones. The dark, secret weight of it, the beauty.

She tore her eyes away at last and began walking along by the glass cases, dazed by the sight of hundreds of jars, each containing a different animal, floating in clear liquid. There were more rooms off the main hall, and she slipped into one to find more glass cases and wide drawers that lit up when she opened them. Inside were thousands of shells, arranged in rows. Line upon line of whorled, ridged treasures, each a tiny kingdom...

They found her nearly an hour later, the museum in an uproar, everyone looking. Her name had been announced half a dozen times on the public-address system, but Stella had been too lost in wonder to hear.

That evening, back at home, she stood silently in the doorway of Deb's room, watching her pack her suitcase.

'I shouldn't have taken my eyes off you,' Deb said, jerking a dress off its hanger. 'I wasn't doing my job.'

'It wasn't your fault.' Stella squeezed her hands together until her knuckles were white. 'It really *wasn't*.'

Deb wasn't listening to her. She seemed to be talking to herself.

'All the same, I can't do everything. Grief or no grief, a dad ought to spend more time at home...'

She wasn't folding her clothes. She was just bunching them up and shoving them into the suitcase.

Deb shook her head. 'It isn't right!'

Stella didn't understand what 'it' was, but the word made her feel uneasy. As if 'it' was code for something so terrible that it couldn't be named.

Later she went to the spare room and sat for a long time looking at the painting of the sea, trying to remember her mum's face. She thought of the skeleton of the whale, of the great hollow space where its heart had been, and tears filled her eyes.

It isn't right!

None of it would have happened, Stella thought, if she'd just shown the man her necklace. So maybe 'it' wasn't really an 'it' at all.

Maybe 'it' was Stella.

four

Stella began spending every lunch break in the school library. She liked it there. She didn't have to feel ashamed that she had nobody to talk to, because in the library nobody was allowed to talk anyway.

One day she came across a book about coral reefs. It had a photo of waves breaking against rocks, and another of dolphins moving through the water like silver stitches running through blue silk. Stella took a long time reading the book, then she slipped it into her bag when nobody was looking. A week later, she discovered an encyclopedia full of drawings of shells, and she took that too.

She didn't know why she stole the books. She did it on impulse, and she kept it a secret.

One day she found a book of folk tales in the history section of the library. There was a picture of a mermaid on the cover. Stella stood still in the narrow passageway between the bookshelves. It was so quiet she could hear the hum of traffic on the distant motorway, the tiny sound of her finger against the pages as she traced the picture's outline.

The mermaid looked slightly — very slightly — like her mum.

According to legend, mermaids could bring on storms and tell the future, she read. *Some were sirens, luring sailors to their doom; others had mysterious healing powers. All were beautiful, with flowing hair and graceful features. They liked nothing better than to perch on rocks, admiring their reflections, or to glide through their underwater kingdoms, strewn with jewels and treasure—*

Stella closed the book and quickly stuffed it into her bag. She took it home and put it under her bed, along with the encyclopedia of shells, and the book about coral reefs.

She hid them right at the back, next to the wall, for fear Mrs Chapman would find them. Mrs Chapman was always tidying, and you could tell how she was feeling just by watching her clean. When she was angry, her vacuum cleaner left crisscrossed lines all over the carpet. Yet in a good mood, she sorted the cutlery drawer as if putting the whole world to rights.

She always dusted Stella's bedroom slowly, pausing at the photograph of Stella's mum on the bedside table.

'Beautiful,' she would say. 'Too beautiful for this world, and that's a fact.'

And she would wipe the face behind the glass as gently as if it were a real one.

Mrs Chapman was kept even busier when Stella's grandmother arrived to live in the small apartment at the top of the house. Stella liked Gramma. She was tall and always perfectly dressed and, like Stella, she had a tendency to drift.

Gramma forgot things, and then she forgot she had forgotten them and suddenly remembered them again. Her memories didn't follow each other in order; they were more like a well-shuffled deck of cards. There was no way of telling which would come out on top.

Every day after school, Stella climbed the stairs

to Gramma's apartment and drank tea out of her teacups with the blue rims.

'How lovely to see you!' Gramma said, sounding surprised, whenever Stella appeared at her door.

She sat on the sofa knitting, although no matter how much time she spent, the knitting never seemed to grow. It was as if all her stitches somehow undid themselves overnight, so next day she was back where she started.

'What are you making?' Stella asked.

'A dear little sweater for Anthony,' Gramma said.

'For Dad? Isn't it a bit small?' Stella said, looking at the tiny sleeve.

'Well,' Gramma said calmly, 'I expect it will stretch.'

Gramma had such a kind, untroubled face that Stella felt she could tell her anything.

'Do you think I'm strange, Gramma?' she asked one day.

Gramma smiled. 'Isn't everyone?'

Stella shook her head. 'Most people are... normal.'

'That's only because you don't know them.' Gramma poured her another cup of tea, the liquid clear and golden in the white china cup. 'In my opinion, the more you know a person, the stranger they become.'

'I stole three books from the library and hid them under my bed,' Stella said.

'How unusual.'

'I don't even know why I did it,' Stella said. 'One was a book about shells, one was about coral reefs, and I took the last one because it had a mermaid on the cover.'

As she said the word 'mermaid', a memory came to Stella. It was so clear and fully formed that it felt as though it had always been there, just below the surface of her mind. The memory was of her mum. She was sitting on the window seat, with her knees drawn up and her bare feet resting on the padded fabric.

Stella's mum had had extremely large feet for her height. They looked, Stella often thought, as if they didn't quite belong to her. It was why she had been so accident prone, forever tripping over things…

In the memory, Stella was standing next to the window, and she must have been very young because her head only came up to the level of her mum's hands. She was showing her mum something in a book. It was a picture of a mermaid. Her mum looked down at the page.

'There's no such thing,' she said.

Stella wasn't sure why she remembered this tiny incident, out of all the thousands of others. Maybe it had stuck in her mind because her mum's voice had sounded different. Not sharp — her mum was never sharp — but unusually abrupt. Or maybe it was the way Stella had felt in that moment. As if she had done something wrong without knowing quite what.

But whatever the reason for the memory, now that it had come it wouldn't go away.

Stella thought about it as she stared out of the window of the school bus, watching the flat land speed by. Perhaps Mrs Chapman was right. Her mum had never belonged here. She had belonged somewhere else; in a world that was beautiful enough even for her. She had belonged to the sea.

A mermaid! Stella thought.

Then she stopped and shook her head. She was letting her mind wander again, she was *drifting*. Stella forced her gaze away from the window, back to the interior of the bus, and the empty seat beside her.

A mermaid? she thought. How did she come up with such stupid things? No wonder nobody ever wanted to sit next to her.

five

Cam arrived in Stella's life when she turned twelve. The school year had already begun, and nobody was expecting a new girl to join the class. The day before she came was like any other.

Stella got off the bus after school, and walked down the street like she always did, passing the identical houses with their neat front gardens and tidy driveways. She unlocked the door and stepped into the hallway.

Tina, her current nanny, was in the front room. She looked up from her phone as Stella came in.

'Hi! How was your day?'

'Good,' Stella said.

'Awesome!' Tina said, with her big, automatic smile. 'Got much homework?'

'Not too much.'

'Awesome!' Tina said again. She thought a lot of things were awesome. It was her favourite word.

'Let me know if you need help with anything,' she said, already glancing back at her phone.

Stella dumped her bag and went up the stairs to Gramma's apartment.

'Stella!' Gramma cried. 'How lovely to see you!'

Stella hugged her.

'How about some tea?'

'I think Mrs Chapman is already making it,' Stella said, hearing the clatter of kettle and cups in the kitchenette.

Gramma patted the sofa. 'Come and sit next to me.'

Mrs Chapman came through the door with a tray. 'Thank you,' Gramma said, looking at her with polite curiosity. 'I don't think we've been introduced... are you new?'

'It's Mrs Chapman,' Stella reminded her. 'She makes tea for us every afternoon.'

'How kind!' Gramma declared. 'What a lovely thing to do!'

Stella poured them each a cup of tea. 'Tell me a story,' she begged. 'Tell me about when you were little and you went to the seaside, and your bracelet fell off in the water, and you couldn't find it. Did you go to the sea a lot, Gramma? What's it like?'

'Well, it's blue, of course,' Gramma said vaguely. 'Full of salt, you know.

It was such a lovely bracelet,' she continued. 'It had belonged to my own grandmother. The stones were semi-precious, all different. My mother thought I was far too young to wear such a thing, and certainly not in the water, but I didn't do what I was told and—'

She broke off. 'Where's Anthony today?'

'Dad's away. He'll be back tonight.'

'Away? Yes, of course, the school trip. I hope he remembers to brush his teeth. He'd have fur growing on them if I didn't remind him.'

Stella tried to imagine her quiet, serious dad with furry teeth. She couldn't. 'He's grown up now,' she told Gramma. 'He's forty-two years old.'

'Is he?' Gramma beamed. 'How wonderful.'

Her grandmother was a time traveller, Stella thought. She was always arriving — with great delight and surprise — into her own future.

'Why don't you tell me about your day?' Gramma said.

Stella sighed and leaned her head against Gramma's shoulder, soft wool brushing her cheek. 'It was just the same...'

Gramma squeezed her hand. 'Things will change.'

'How do you know?'

'Because they always do,' Gramma said.

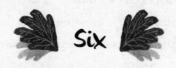

Six

Gramma was right. Things did change, and the change was Cam.

'This is Camille Jenkins,' the teacher said. 'Please welcome her to the class.'

The girl didn't act like a new kid. She didn't smile, or give an embarrassed little wave, or look down at her feet.

'It's Ca*milla*,' she said. And then she walked to the back of the room, and sat down in the spare seat next to Stella.

Stella looked at her out of the corner of her eye. Her clothes were different, and her height, and even the colour of her skin.

The girl opened her bag and took out her pens and notebook, tossing them noisily on to the desk, as if she hadn't noticed — or didn't care — that everyone was staring at her. Stella felt a surge of admiration. She racked her brains for something interesting or funny to say.

'I like your pencil case,' she finally murmured.

The girl didn't answer, and Stella wondered if she'd heard, or whether she was ignoring her. At the front of the class, the teacher was handing out books. 'We're going to be reading *The Lord of the Flies*,' she announced.

'I read that at my last school,' the girl told Stella.

'Really?' Stella flushed with surprise.

'It's exactly the same as *The Lord of the Rings*.'

Stella stared at her uncertainly.

'Except instead of hobbits, all the characters are bugs. Swear on my life.'

'There's nothing to laugh about, Stella Martin!' the teacher scolded.

Stella didn't care. She'd never had someone to laugh with at the back of English class before. Or any class, for that matter.

'Her name is *Camilla*,' she told Gramma over tea

that day. 'Only she said to call her Cam. You'll never guess how many schools she's been to — six! She has a brother and a dog called Bubble, and her mum and dad dig up things.'

'Dig up things?'

'Old things, pottery, stuff like that. It's why she's been to so many schools, because her parents keep hearing of new places to dig around in.'

'How odd,' Gramma remarked. She smiled. 'It sounds as if you two really hit it off.'

'I didn't talk much,' Stella admitted, 'but it didn't matter. Cam talks a *lot*.'

Cam was quick to say something was boring. She sat next to Stella on the school bus, staring at the fields stretching into the distance.

'I don't know why we bother looking out of the window,' she said. 'What's the point? Everything's the same. Same, same, same. It's like watching paint dry.

Only in slow motion,' she added.

'I know what you mean,' Stella said. 'There's too much space, and too much sky. Sometimes it makes me feel... like I can't breathe.'

The moment the words were out of her mouth, she regretted them. Cam raised her eyebrows.

'You're not the same, same, same,' she said. 'You're weird.'

Stella's chest felt hollow, as if her heart had suddenly shrunk. She stared down at her lap.

'I know I am,' she said.

Cam burst out laughing. 'Not weird-weird,' she said. 'Weird-*interesting*.'

It was one of the nicest things anyone had ever said about her, Stella thought.

Cam came to Stella's house after school one day, and by the Christmas holidays she was coming a couple of times a week. They did their homework together, although Stella often copied Cam's answers because Cam finished way ahead, and then spent the rest of the time trying to distract her.

'What does Tina actually do all day?' she asked. 'Why do you call Mrs Chapman, "Mrs Chapman"? Is it because she has a really embarrassing first name, like Frumtilda?'

'Frumtilda isn't even a name,' Stella said.

'That's probably what Mrs Chapman thinks too,' Cam said. 'Poor old Frumtilda...'

Sometimes Cam lay on the floor in Stella's bedroom, and read out loud from her own diary.

November 11th

Mum and Dad were droning on and on about some boring old jug handle they found. I can't believe they are really my parents. I've spent AGES looking for evidence that I'm adopted, but no luck. So far. At lunch, a rat was running around the canteen only it turned out it was only Ben Fassberg's squeaky shoes. Why does nothing exciting ever happen???

'I thought you weren't supposed to tell anyone what you wrote in your diary,' Stella said.

'What would be the point of that?'

Stella shrugged. 'I don't know, so you could keep it a secret? That's what I'd do, anyway.'

Cam's face immediately lit up. 'What secrets do you have? Tell me!'

'I don't, I was just saying…'

'I bet you do.'

'I do *not*!' Stella protested, although she knew it was a mistake. Cam's teasing always got worse the instant she sensed weakness.

'I don't believe you,' Cam sang. 'You're hiding something. Where is it, Stella? Under your bed?'

'There isn't anything there!' Stella cried. But Cam was already on her knees, her arm reaching.

'If there's nothing there, why are you going red?' Cam stretched her arm further under the bed and pulled out the three stolen books. She grinned with triumph. 'So that's your deep dark secret! Old library books! What do you do with them? Study them at night in guilty secret?'

'No, I don't!'

Cam opened the encyclopedia of shells at random. She held it up so Stella could see the pictures, but not the words.

'What's this one?'

'Zigzag scallop,' Stella said, shamefaced.

'And this?'

'Button shell,' she admitted.

Cam closed the book, shaking her head in disbelief. 'You really *are* weird.'

'I know I am,' Stella said. It was what she always said when Cam told her she was weird, which was quite often. It had become their private joke.

You're weird!

I know I am!

Stella smiled. She glanced at the other library

books, her gaze falling on the cover of the book of folk tales.

'I used to think my mum was a mermaid...' she said. 'Ages and ages ago,' she added hastily.

Cam shrugged. 'I used to think my mum was a witch. And I still do.'

They turned back to their homework, the conversation already half-forgotten. And Stella may never have remembered it if Gramma hadn't gone time travelling again.

Seven

Gramma was always forgetful, but recently she seemed to be getting worse. She had lost her glasses three times the day before, even though they were hanging on a plastic chain around her neck. Then she thought Stella's nanny, Tina, was a stranger who had wandered into the house by mistake.

'She didn't look as if she knew what she was doing,' Gramma told Stella.

It was surprising, Stella thought, how often Gramma got things right, without even realising it.

She wanted to ask Cam if she'd noticed anything different about Gramma, but Cam had problems of her own.

'My parents are driving me crazy,' she said, as they lay in the spring sunshine on the school playing field. 'They keep breaking off their conversation whenever I come into the room. As if they've been discussing some big secret.'

She paused, her eyes narrowed. 'I think they're getting a divorce. Either that or a pony for my birthday.'

'I hope it's a pony,' Stella said.

Cam stretched her long legs. 'A pony would be too small. Perhaps it's a horse instead.'

'Where would you keep it?' Stella asked, thinking of Cam's pocket-sized garden.

Cam ignored the question. 'I think I'll ride it to school instead of going on the bus,' she said. 'It could graze here on the playing field while I'm in class.

Its poop could fertilise the grass,' she added.

Stella laughed, although she was still worried about Gramma. The moment she got home from school, she went upstairs to see her.

'Stella! What a lovely surprise!'

Gramma was wearing her cardigan inside out. She had never done that before. But anyone could make that kind of mistake, Stella told herself. Once she had gone to school with her skirt on back to front, and not even noticed until lunchtime.

Stella sat down on the sofa.

Her grandmother appeared distracted. She was pottering around the room, looking in the corners.

'What's the matter, Gramma?'

'I have to get ready. Have you seen my shoes? The silver ones?'

Stella shook her head.

'I need them,' Gramma said. 'Anthony is getting married today to such a lovely girl.'

She was talking about Stella's mum. Gramma had gone back in time again, to the day of Stella's mum's wedding.

'A lovely girl,' Gramma repeated. 'Do you want to know a secret?'

Stella stared at her uneasily. Gramma was far away, more fixed in the past than ever before.

'I… guess so,' she faltered.

'She used to be a mermaid,' Gramma said in a voice so low it was practically a whisper. 'Now what do you think of *that*?'

Stella's whole body went still.

'There's no need to look so surprised,' Gramma

said. 'It's perfectly true. I saw it with my own eyes.'

Was her grandmother making fun of her? But Gramma never teased, she was far too kind for that.

'A beautiful tail and everything,' Gramma declared, smiling at the memory.

'Where was this?' Stella said, finding her voice.

'We were on holiday,' Gramma murmured. 'An island, I forget the name. End something or other... no... that's not it...' Her voice trailed off.

Stella almost cried out in frustration. She jumped up and tugged at Gramma's arm. 'But what did you actually see? Are you sure it was her?'

Gramma looked flustered. 'Who?'

'My *mum*. Please try to remember, Gramma!'

'I can't.' Gramma shook her head in desperation. 'I *can't*.'

'But you were talking about it a moment ago!'

'It's just like when I lost my bracelet in the ocean,' Gramma said softly. 'I tried to dive for it. But it's so quiet underwater; you wonder where the sound went. And your eyes play tricks on you. It's hard to tell the distance between things.'

Her grandmother looked so upset that Stella took her hand and squeezed it gently.

'Don't worry, Gramma, it's okay...'

'The bracelet looks so close,' Gramma said, her voice small and sad. 'But I can't reach it, no matter how much I try.'

Eight

Stella went to her room and sat down heavily on the bed, gazing at the photograph on the bedside table. The way Gramma had talked — as if her mum was actually there — had made it feel for a moment as if she was still alive, and Stella was caught by a wave of grief and longing. She'd thought she'd got used to missing her mum, but she hadn't. The feeling was as strong, and as terrible as it had ever been.

Why had Gramma said she was a mermaid? What had she meant by it?

Gramma muddled everything up, Stella told herself. It was no use trying to make sense of anything she said.

She picked up the photograph, fingering the stone around her neck as she stared in concentration at her mum's image. Her head and shoulders were at a slight angle, with her face turned towards the camera, and her hair flowed down her back in a fiery wave. Stella peered at the background, hoping to find some detail that she'd missed before. But it was only a pale, fuzzy blur. The picture had been taken in a studio. They had left the background out of focus on purpose, so it wouldn't distract from her mum's face.

Gramma muddled everything up, Stella thought. But she didn't *make* things up. In her own way, she was the most truthful person that Stella knew.

She turned the photograph over. The back of the frame hadn't been opened in a long time, and the hooks were stiff. Stella removed the glass cautiously, and then the photograph itself.

She hadn't really been expecting to find anything, and sure enough, she didn't. Just a sheet of white cardboard with a rectangle cut out of it, and another, thinner sheet to keep the photo in place. It was only when she was returning the pieces to the frame that Stella discovered that there was one of her mum's drawings on the back of the second sheet of cardboard.

She caught her breath.

It was a pencil sketch of a mermaid.

Below the drawing, in her mum's handwriting, were the words:

Crystal Cove, Lastland Island.

The sketch was about ten centimetres high, and had been made with a few quick lines, although the head of the mermaid had been drawn in much more detail.

It was delicate-looking, fine-boned, surrounded by a wispy cloud of hair. Her nose was long, and her heavy-lidded eyes held a faraway gaze, as if the owner of the face was lost in some memory. If so, it was perhaps not a completely happy one, for there was a hint of discontent in the line of her narrow mouth, and something impatient in the way she held her body, as though she was longing to turn away, but for some reason couldn't.

One hand was raised, the palm flat and rigid. Was she waving, Stella wondered, or gesturing in protest? Neither explanation seemed quite right.

The drawing was odd in another way too, although it took Stella a moment before she worked out why. She had seen many images of mermaids, and while they varied widely — realistic-looking or cartoony, mysteriously beautiful or childishly cute, they were alike in one important detail. They were all images of *something* — a mermaid — rather than *someone*.

But this drawing was different. There was nothing generic or standard about it. The face was far too individual for that. It was a portrait. Her mum hadn't made it up, or copied it from a book.

She had drawn a picture of somebody *real*.

Nine

Next day, Stella couldn't wait to tell Cam about the drawing and what Gramma had told her, although when it came to it, she didn't know quite how to begin.

'Gramma said something really strange yesterday,' she ventured.

Cam smiled. 'I love your Gramma. She says the funniest things.'

Stella hesitated, and then tried again.

'Do you remember me telling you I used to think my mum was a mermaid?'

Cam shook her head.

'I know only little kids believe stuff like that,' Stella

said. 'I mean, I knew it wasn't true or anything, but then Gramma said Mum *was*. She said she'd actually seen her. She said she had a tail and everything.'

'Wow!' Cam said.

'I know, right?' Stella said, feeling encouraged. 'I thought it was just Gramma getting muddled, but then I found one of Mum's old drawings.'

She pulled it out of her bag and handed it to Cam.

Cam examined the picture. 'Your mum was really good at art.'

'Doesn't that look like someone... *real*?' Stella asked.

In her head it all fitted together, like pieces of a story. The way Gramma had spoken, despite her confusion, and the eerily life-like quality of Mum's drawing. The way she swam, and had taught Stella to swim, talking to her all the time: *You moved through water before you were born, all you have to do is remember.* There was her beauty, her difference, her painting of the ocean, that look on her face when she'd said there were no such things as mermaids, the necklace with a stone she called the word of the sea. And every story about mermaids seemed to end with loss and desertion and death. So that was part of it too.

All this flashed through Stella's mind in an instant. But she couldn't find the right words.

'I thought… I don't know, it's just strange, like too much of a coincidence,' she said. 'I mean, what if Gramma is right?'

'You could have relatives who are mermaids, or mermen, or whatever they're called,' Cam said.

'*Merpeople*!' she added.

'So you *do* think she might be right?' Stella said eagerly. Too late, she saw the expression on Cam's face. Cam believed her, but only in the way she believed she was getting a horse for her birthday, or that she was adopted, or that someone's squeaky shoes might actually be a rat running around the school: because it was fun to believe things like that, because Cam liked to be dramatic and funny and *interesting*.

Cam stared at her for a second, then started laughing.

'You really think your mum was a mermaid? You really mean it?'

'I didn't say she was! I only said *might*…'

Cam laughed even louder.

'I only said *might*!' Stella's face flushed. She snatched the drawing from Cam's hand.

'Hey,' Cam said. 'Why are you getting so upset?' She was still smirking, though. She was still laughing at Stella inside. The school bus was pulling up. Brakes hissed and kids jostled, pushing to be first on.

'I'll go there, to Lastland Island, you'll see,' Stella said furiously. 'One day I'll go there and find out.'

She couldn't stop thinking about the way Cam had laughed, so loudly, so hilariously. Cam hadn't laughed just because she thought Stella's theory was ridiculous; that would have been bad enough. What had made her really crack up was the fact that Stella actually believed it. And that felt far worse.

Ten

Stella was late next morning and missed the bus. Mrs Chapman had to drive her to school, so she didn't see Cam until later, by the lockers.

'I have major news,' Cam announced, as if she had completely forgotten about their argument.

'Really?' Stella said, her voice flat. Cam's news was always 'major', no matter how petty it turned out to be. The bell rang, putting an end to any conversation, and Stella trailed off to class without another word.

She didn't see Cam again until lunchtime, when Cam sat opposite her in the canteen. Now Cam was strangely quiet. She stared at her plate of chicken, making track marks in the sauce with her fork.

'It's not a divorce *or* a pony,' she said.

'What d'you mean?'

'My parents. Their big secret. It's a new job.'

Stella stared at her.

'We're moving,' Cam said.

On the other side of the table, a boy flicked a piece of broccoli off his plate, and a girl pushed back her chair with an outraged shriek.

'You mean, like, to another house?' Stella faltered.

'Another *town*,' Cam said, naming a place Stella had never heard of. 'It's on the coast.'

'That's... hundreds of miles away.'

Cam nodded. 'It's a really big deal for my parents, they say we won't have to move again for ages.' She was talking even faster than usual. 'We're going at the start of next week, the removal guys are coming to take our stuff so it's there when we arrive.'

'Next week?' Stella repeated. She wanted to shout: *You can't go! You have to tell them you can't!* But the memory of Cam's laughter got in the way.

'I wish it wasn't so soon,' Cam said.

Stella thought she would cry, yet she didn't. She sat through the rest of lunch, and English class, and all the way home on the bus, carrying her tears inside her, afraid they would spill if she moved too fast, or spoke too loudly.

At home, she went to the spare room, and sat staring at the painting of the ocean, her mind as bleak and empty as the picture itself.

'Are you okay, Stellabella?' Her dad was hovering in the doorway.

For a second, Stella thought of telling him what had happened. But although her dad had met Cam, and spoken with her from time to time, he didn't really know what she meant to Stella. She could try to explain it to him, but what would be the point, when Cam was leaving in a few days anyway?

It wasn't until she was having tea with Gramma that the tears finally came.

'My poor darling,' Gramma said, putting an arm around her. 'You have a good cry, get it all out.'

Her grandmother had lost so much, Stella thought. Her years mixed up, her memories scrambled. Yet her kindness was still there. The more she lost, the more the kindness showed, like a rock on the beach when the tide was going out.

Stella pressed her face against Gramma's arm and cried even harder.

Eleven

Over the next few days, as the school year wound down, Stella grew quieter and quieter, and the less she said, the more talkative Cam became.

'Mum says it will take nearly two days to drive to the new place,' she chattered frantically. 'Can you imagine? Nearly two whole days in the car with smelly Bubble! I'll *die*, swear on my life. How can an animal that tiny stink so bad?'

Cam talked so much about the move that Stella began to think she couldn't wait to leave. They sat on the school bus and Cam described the packing she had to do, her new school, her new house. The house had a porch — she'd seen a picture. It was on the outskirts of town, barely a mile from the sea.

Outside, on the long straight road, pools of heat shimmered black. The clouds were scratch marks on the hard surface of the sky. Stella leaned her head against the wall of the bus, sick with misery and envy.

A mile was no distance. Cam would be able to see the ocean just by looking out of her bedroom window. No wonder she was glad to leave.

'I'll really, really miss you,' Cam said for the hundredth time. 'But we'll still talk to each other. We'll talk every single day, for hours, won't we?'

Cam exaggerated everything, Stella thought, you couldn't rely on a word she said. Hadn't she pretended to believe Stella's story about mermaids?

At home, Tina was lying on her back on the living room floor, with her phone in the air, taking a selfie.

'Hi!' she called out as Stella went by. 'How was your day?'

'Awesome,' Stella said.

Tina opened her mouth and then shut it again. 'Oh… good,' she said, sounding confused.

Cam might be leaving, but there was still Gramma. Stella could visit her to chat and drink tea, just like she always did. She hadn't shown Gramma the drawing of the mermaid yet, and it occurred to her that the sight of it might jog her memory. Perhaps Gramma would be able to tell her more, or at least explain what she had meant by her strange words. Stella went to her room and opened the drawer in the bedside table where she had hidden the drawing.

She stared at the image. The more she thought about it, the more convinced she became that it held the key to Gramma's memory. Her hand trembled a little, and she took a deep breath to steady herself. But all the way up the stairs to Gramma's apartment, she could feel her heart pattering faster and faster.

She knocked on the door and waited for what seemed like a long time. She was about to lift her hand to knock again, when the door opened.

'I've got something to show you,' Stella said in a rush. Then she stopped.

Gramma looked different, taller, and yet somehow further away. She smiled at Stella.

Something was terribly wrong. Gramma's smile was uncertain, oddly polite.

'Hello?' Gramma said, making it sound like a question. 'Are you here to visit someone?'

Stella's grandmother forgot a lot of things. She forgot the years, and what she had just said, and who people were. But she didn't forget Stella. She *couldn't*.

'It's me,' Stella said. 'It's *me*.'

Gramma's smile faded, her face was puzzled.

'I live here,' Stella said, her voice beginning to shake. 'I see you every day.'

Gramma looked even more puzzled. 'How nice...' she said. Then she brightened. 'You must be a friend of Anthony's!'

'Dad's grown up,' Stella whispered.

'You look so sad. Why, you're crying! Has Anthony done something to upset you?' Gramma's voice was full of concern. 'He doesn't always know the right thing to say, you know. But he has a very good heart...

You mustn't worry,' she added. 'Everything will be all right.'

Stella shook her head. 'It won't... it can't...'

She turned and ran downstairs, the world so bright and broken by her tears that she could hardly see where she was going.

Back in her room, she sat numbly on the edge of the bed, her face wet. Cam was leaving the day after tomorrow. Stella might never see her again. And now even Gramma looked at her as if she was a stranger.

There was nobody in the world left to talk to.

Twelve

Stella was still holding the drawing. She looked down at it blankly. Cam had been right to laugh at her, she thought. Only a child of five would wonder whether her mum had been a mermaid or not. And even then, the child of five would have to be pretty stupid. The sort of child, Stella told herself, who caused people to shake their heads and whisper behind their hands.

Away with the fairies, poor little thing, such a terrible shame.

Stella sniffed and wiped her eyes, trying to pull herself together. Her gaze returned to the words below her mum's drawing.

Crystal Cove, Lastland Island.

Gramma had mentioned an island, although she hadn't remembered the name of it. 'End something,' she'd said.

Could she have meant 'Lastland'? Stella sat up straight.

She must have done.

Lastland Island wasn't something Stella's mum had made up for fun. It was an actual place. And if Lastland Island was real, then maybe the rest of it was real too.

Stella leaped over to her desk. She looked up the name, and quickly found the island on the map. It was a speck in the blue, a few miles off the mainland. She scanned the coast and saw there was a town directly opposite, separated from the island by a narrow strip of sea. Her eyes widened.

It was the town that Cam was moving to.

Sometimes a coincidence is so extraordinary, so incredibly unlikely, that it's hard to believe it can possibly be random. Instead it feels like fate. The instant Stella realised that the town on the map was the same one that Cam's family was heading to, she felt certainty flood through her.

It was meant to be.

Cam had talked so much about the move to her new home that Stella had stopped listening. Now she ransacked her mind for the details. Tomorrow was Friday; Cam and her family were leaving on Saturday morning, and the journey would take nearly two days. But their furniture and possessions were being taken separately – the removal van was due to come the day before the family left...

It didn't take long to pack. To avoid suspicion, Stella thought it best to take only what would fit into her school bag. A change of clothes, a torch, five protein bars, two apples, a large bottle of water, a comb, a toothbrush and toothpaste and a month's worth of saved-up pocket money. She added the book of folk tales as an afterthought. Two days was a long time, she might be glad of something to read.

The money wasn't nearly enough, but Stella decided she would worry about that later. She had made up her mind. She was running away.

She was going to Lastland Island to find out whether her mum had been a mermaid or not. Because if she had been, then what exactly did that make Stella?

Thirteen

I t was pitch dark, and so hot, even Stella's eyelids felt sticky.

She lay curled up on Cam's mum's new sofa, horribly worried in case she left sweaty stains all over the blue velvet. Cam's mum was very particular about her sofa. She didn't allow Cam to sit on it, in case Cam made scuff marks or spilled something, or just breathed on it in the wrong way.

'If me and that sofa were about to fall off a cliff, my mum would save the sofa,' Cam had said. 'It's the truth, swear on my life.'

Stella knew she shouldn't be lying on the sofa, but there was nowhere else to be. Every centimetre of the removal van was crammed with furniture, household items and cardboard boxes. They were packed so tight that even when the van turned a corner or hit a bump, nothing moved, except a piece of loose china buried in one of the boxes to Stella's right, which made a tiny ringing noise that sounded like a cry.

Whereare we going, whereare we going? it sang, over and over again.

Stella covered her ears with her hands, fighting the temptation to check the time again. No matter how long she waited before glancing at the luminous green face of her watch, only four minutes would have passed since the last time she looked.

It had been easier than she thought to sneak into the removal van. She'd got ready for school that morning as she always did, except that before she went to catch the bus, she left her phone behind on her desk, and a note under her pillow.

I haven't been kidnapped, the note read. *Please don't worry. I will be back in a few days.*

She left the house, but instead of heading for the bus stop, she turned in the other direction and walked to

Cam's house. The removal van was already there. The back was rolled up, and two men were busy trundling items to and fro. Stella waited until they were inside the house at the same time, and then made a dash for the back of the van, hiding in the narrow gap behind the sofa while they carried on with their work.

After nearly three hours on the road, the driver pulled over to take a break. Stella heard both cab doors slam, and the sound of footsteps, then nothing for what seemed like ages, except the tremble and whoosh of passing vehicles.

She felt around in her bag for a protein bar and an apple, ate them slowly, and took a long drink of water. The bottle felt far lighter than it had. She turned on her torch and saw that the bottle was half-empty already. She would have to ration it more carefully. Just the thought of running out of water frightened her. Stella knew that panic wasn't far away. It was with her in the van, one shade darker than the darkness itself, and each hour brought it closer.

The van started up again, and this time drove for so long that Stella dozed and finally fell asleep.

She woke up a couple of hours later, not knowing where she was, her heart pounding. She reached out, found the back of the sofa and remembered she was in the removal van, running away from home, with only four protein bars and an apple left to eat.

On top of that, she was desperate to pee. She took out her torch and her book in an effort to distract herself, but it was no use.

Then she realised she could use her by now empty water bottle.

Stella was so pleased at overcoming the problem that she decided to have another protein bar to celebrate. She turned back to her book.

There was once a man who played the pipe so merrily, she read, *that even the fish danced. One day a mermaid came up from the depths of the sea to listen. The moment he saw her, the man fell instantly in love…*

Stella turned the page.

A selkie is a seal that can take human form. But if she loses her sealskin, she must stay on land until she finds it. It's said that selkies love music, and many a night on lonely beaches and wild, rocky shores, one may hear them singing with voices as pure and haunting as the moonlight itself…

Ringed by the shifting halo of the torch, the words took on new mystery and depth. There was so much Stella didn't understand. She had never even seen the sea with her own eyes. Knowing she would be there soon made her feel breathless with excitement.

Just before midnight, the van stopped for the night. The beam of Stella's torch had grown yellowish, and she switched it off, fearful of the battery running out. Darkness pressed against her.

There were no windows or vents in the back of the van, and the air had grown stale. Stella wondered what would happen if she ran out of oxygen, and the more she wondered, the harder it became to breathe. She rested the palms of her hands against her chest, feeling the shape of her necklace, and thought about the sea instead. She was on her way; she would get there soon.

In a little while her heart grew quiet, and her breathing slowed. She closed her eyes and tried as hard as she could to go to sleep.

The van was back on the road next morning and didn't slow down until almost midday. It turned left, and then right, left again, and each time it turned, the loose piece of china cried out in protest.

Hurts meso bad, hurts meso bad!

Stella's body ached and her head spun. The heat and the darkness and the worry had become almost more than she could bear, and she was wondering how much longer she could hold on without screaming, when the van finally pulled over and stopped.

A moment later, she heard the steely rattle of the back rolling up. Stella crouched low on the sofa. A wall of cardboard boxes — five layers deep — lay between her hiding place and daylight so bright, it was enough to half-blind her.

Something banged, and one of the men cursed.

'Ramp's jammed!'

'Let's get the smaller stuff, do the rest later,' the other suggested.

Stella scrambled over the back of the sofa, moving as fast as her stiff limbs would allow. The air was even staler there and her breath came short and shallow.

She heard the slide of cardboard as the first layer of boxes was removed. Then the floor of the van shook. One of the men had climbed inside.

'I'll hand them down, okay?'

He sounded close. She could hear the slightest shift of his feet, and the low grunt he made as he lifted.

'Heavy one here.'

Stella hadn't given much thought to how she would escape from the van without being seen. She wondered if she could crawl deeper into the furniture behind. But it was packed too tightly for that.

'It's hot,' the man standing in the van complained. 'How about a break?'

They clattered across the back of the van, and Stella heard them thump down into the street, their footsteps fading. For a second, she was too paralysed with relief to move. Then she shoved against the sofa, throwing her full weight behind it. Grabbing her bag, she tiptoed to the end of the van and peered out.

The man with the phone was standing on the pavement with his back turned. There was no sign of the other. Stella took a deep breath and clambered down. She crept around the side of the van, and took off along the street, walking as fast as she could.

fourteen

The street was wide, with houses set behind trees. When Stella got to the first crossroad, she turned left without hesitation, not wanting to look as if she didn't know where she was going. Then she stopped to think about what to do next. She could wait for Cam to get there, although Cam and her family had only set off that morning, and wouldn't arrive until tomorrow at the earliest. Besides, Stella didn't want to see Cam. Cam had laughed at her mermaid idea. She would think Stella mad to have run away because of it. Mad and ridiculous…

A breeze picked up, carrying a sharp, briny scent that instantly drove all other thought from Stella's mind.

The sea! She just knew it was that.

She began to walk in the direction where the breeze was coming from, her legs still wobbly from her long journey in the van. The houses thinned and the road began to wind uphill. At the top it curved into one last bend, then levelled to reveal the view.

The broad, blue banner of the sea suddenly stretched out below. Stella stopped short, the breeze on her face, her hand at the stone around her neck. How vast the ocean looked, how cleanly the horizon cut the sky, how bright the water glittered!

She'd thought it would be like coming to the end of the world, but it wasn't like that. It was like coming to where the world began.

She began to walk downhill, slowly at first, then faster and faster, and by the time she was halfway down, she was running, hair flying, backpack bouncing against her shoulders. The road forked when it reached the bottom, leading towards a group of houses on the left, and on the right in the direction of what was clearly the town, some way in the distance.

In between, separated from the road by a low line of grassy dunes, lay the beach.

Without hesitating, Stella clambered over the dunes and into the soft sand beyond. The breeze was stronger on the beach. She could hear the steady pulse of the surf as it beat against the shore, and the long, muttering intake of its breath as it drew back again. She walked towards the water, to where the sand glistened and the waves broke white.

Raising her hand to shield her eyes, she squinted along the long beach. A woman sat on a towel, and a child carrying a bucket ran fitfully to and fro. Apart from them, the beach was empty. Stella unlaced her trainers, and pulled off her grubby socks. Then she hesitated.

She had never forgotten her nightmare, all those years ago. Her fear of water had never lost its force. But the sea was *so* beautiful and, besides, she would only be paddling... Stella took a cautious step into the surf.

Up close, the water looked even bluer than it had from the top of the hill. Once, Stella had asked her nanny, Deb, why the sea was that colour.

'I suppose it's because of the sky,' Deb had said. 'The water reflects it.'

But now Stella could see that Deb had been wrong. The blue of the sea wasn't a reflection. It belonged only to itself, and every other blue in the world was borrowed from it. There were a thousand words for that blue, she thought, and not a single one was right. A thousand words for what she was feeling, standing there, with the water tugging at her ankles. But none of those were right either.

The feeling was like the blue. It belonged only to itself. And every other feeling in the world was borrowed from it.

Stella stepped forward, as if in a dream, the foam surging above her knees. How strange the water felt against her skin. Now that she had become used to the cold, she was aware of another sensation, gentle, yet oddly urgent. She cocked her head, listening. It was like voices in a far-off room, she thought, or a swarm of insects half a field away. Something that you sensed was there, although you couldn't quite hear it. A feeling rather than a sound...

She swayed, suddenly dizzy. The horizon was tilting. The sky had narrowed to a tiny strip and the waves had become mountains, shining and rushing and terrible.

'Hey!' piped a voice.

Her trance was broken. The child with the bucket was standing at the edge of the water, staring at her.

'You lookin' for the whale?' he cried.

Stella shook her head. 'What whale?'

She waded out of the water, wringing the hem of her shorts.

'I saw it!' the boy said. 'My mum says I didn't, but I did – I saw the spout of it.' He gestured with his arms. 'Whooooosh.'

'Where?' Stella asked.

'Out there, far out. My mum says there aren't any whales round here, but I *saw* it! It was big. A real big spout. It was *gigantic*!'

He ran off down the beach, his bucket swinging, his head turned to the ocean. Stella watched him for a moment, then fetched her trainers and put them on, and went back over the dunes to the road. She had suddenly realised how hungry she was.

Fifteen

The town was further away than it looked. Stella walked along the coast road for more than two miles before she reached it. It was a sizable place, with a bustling waterfront, and a dock crowded with boats. She spotted a broad white vessel that looked as if it might be a ferry, and went to look at the timetable.

There were departures to Lastland Island listed four times a day. Stella's heart thumped at the sight of the name. She checked her watch. The next ferry was leaving in just over an hour. She found a store selling snacks and souvenirs, bought a packet of biscuits and a bar of chocolate, and sat down on a bench to eat.

Directly opposite, a crowd of tourists clustered in front of a tall, glass-fronted building. It was an aquarium with pictures of turtles and rays decorating the entrance.

Stella had never seen a real turtle or ray before. She hadn't even seen many fish, apart from the glass jars full of pickled specimens in the Natural History Museum. She gazed longingly at the aquarium, knowing she didn't have much money, and should be careful not to waste it.

But was spending money to see turtles and rays really a waste?

To Stella, it suddenly seemed essential.

It was cool and dark in the aquarium. A lady stamped Stella's hand with a tiny fish as she entered and Stella blew on it to dry it. She stood still, taking in the salty smell, and the rows of glowing, illuminated tanks.

At last she set off, pausing for a long time in front of each tank. Many of the names she recognised, from the library book about coral reefs. There were angelfish and chubby puffers, tangs and tetras. How friendly they seemed, following her movements with eyes large and small. Even the giant grouper stirred from the depths of its tank, and rose to stare at her, its huge mouth gaping as she passed by.

She rested the tip of her finger against the glass, and was surprised to see a cluster of frilly guppies instantly swarm to the spot. Living in the aquarium must have made them tame, she thought.

Stella hovered by a large tank of schooling fish, entranced by the hundreds of silver bodies streaming along in the same direction. They never stopped or wavered. They simply kept going, endlessly swimming. She saw her own reflection in the glass, floating in front of the fish. The stone around her neck was glowing slightly in the neon light.

Something flashed, like a mirror shifting towards the sun. Stella blinked. The school of fish was still massed together, still moving at the same steady speed as before.

Except now, they were going the other way.

Why had they changed direction? Stella didn't have time to work it out. She was too distracted by the sight of an even larger tank.

It was circular; she could walk around it on a ramp that spiralled all the way to the top, two floors above. Inside, Stella caught a glimpse of huge silver bodies and the rippling cloak of a manta ray. She peered closer, and suddenly there was a turtle, her massive body filling the glass.

Stella could see each marking on the turtle's ancient shell. She lifted her hand and placed it against the glass, and the turtle turned, her long flippers spread out like wings.

Stella walked further up the ramp.

'Are you following me?' she asked wonderingly. But the turtle only stared at her with its calm, dark eyes.

'I have to catch the ferry,' Stella whispered.

She was thirsty again. She hurried out of the aquarium and returned to the souvenir shop to buy a drink on her way to the dock. The woman at the counter tutted as Stella handed her a note.

'Have you got something smaller?'

Stella shook her head. 'I'm sorry.'

The woman sighed and rummaged in the till drawer. Stella noticed a small TV screen above the counter. It was showing the news, the sound turned down. A reporter was standing on the beach with a microphone, gesturing towards the sea.

Massive whale sighted offshore, read the rolling headline beneath the picture. *Species not yet identified… experts believe the animal may be lost…*

'I can never open these dratted things,' the woman behind the counter said, fumbling with a wrapped up roll of coins.

A new picture flashed on to the TV screen. For a second, Stella was too stunned to make sense of it.

Why is that girl wearing my dress? she thought. *How did that girl get my dress?*

And then: *It's not a girl. It's me.*

Under the photo appeared the words: 'MISSING CHILD'.

The picture changed again. Now Stella saw her dad talking, although she couldn't hear what he was saying. Her dad looked different, older, his face white. Then the photo of Stella returned to the screen.

Stella couldn't tear her eyes away, although she knew she must. She had to. If the woman saw her staring, she might turn to the TV herself, to see what Stella was looking at. And then she would recognise her.

Stella glanced around wildly, saw a display of brightly-coloured caps near the counter, and grabbed one.

'I'll take this too,' she gabbled. 'Don't worry about the change...'

The woman looked startled. She opened her mouth

to say something, although Stella didn't wait to hear. She crammed the cap on her head and bolted.

Back on the street, it was hard not to break into a run. Stella forced herself to keep walking, although her legs were jerky with panic. She ought to have known there would be a nationwide hunt for her. Her photo must have appeared everywhere. Police all over the country were warned and on the watch.

It was a miracle she hadn't been recognised already.

Stella remembered the note she'd left on her desk back at home, and her face burned. *Please don't worry*, she'd written, as if adding the word 'please' would somehow change the fact that everyone was certain to worry, no matter what she wrote. Stella hadn't thought about her dad during the long hours in the removal van. Yet underneath, she'd known that Mrs Chapman would have called him the instant she found Stella missing, and that he would have come home at once, upset, maybe even *frantic*.

She thought of the flat fields and the water towers, and how Gramma had forgotten her. Tears pricked her eyes. She reached into the inside pocket of her jacket and pulled out the drawing of the mermaid, and stared at it for a long time.

She had come so far, and Lastland Island was only a boat ride away.

She tugged the brim of her new cap as low over her face as it would go and counted up the money she had left.

She had enough for a one-way ticket on the ferry, with a little left over.

Sixteen

Stella had imagined Lastland Island would be a
wild place, a lonely outcrop, lashed by waves.
The kind of place where mermaids might
come ashore, carried by high tides and stormy seas.

There was nothing wild about the ferry carrying
her there — it was an ordinary boat, with rows of
plastic-covered seating, and a bar selling hot dogs
and packets of crisps. Stella kept her head down as she
stepped on board, although the man taking tickets
hardly glanced at her.

There were quite a few other passengers on the
ferry. Stella hurried through the main cabin and
found a deserted corner outside, on the lower deck.

Then the engines started, and they were moving out into the bay.

She felt the roll of the vessel beneath her feet, and she could see passengers already walking carefully, at a slight angle. But she felt surprisingly steady, able to keep her balance even with the wind whipping at the hem of her shorts.

She stood at the handrail, not needing to hold, or even touch it. The sky was hazy and the water almost perfectly calm, its surface crosshatched with fine, silvery lines, like etching on a sheet of metal. A patch of reflected light, as bright and as elusive as a sparkler trail, danced a few metres ahead of the ferry, as though leading it on.

Stella looked down. The deck jutted out beyond the ferry's twin hulls, hiding the splash and spray of parting water. All she could see was the surface ahead, still calm and unbroken, speeding by without a ripple.

It was as if they weren't touching the water at all, she thought, but flying over it, carried by an offshore wind towards the open sea.

She leaned over the rail and saw her own shadow, racing along on the surface of the water. Stella knew it was hers; it lifted an arm when she did, and she could see the tiny shape of her necklace dangling clear. But it looked different, thinner, almost sinuous. And the purposeful way it was moving was even more odd. As if it wasn't a shadow, but something separate and alive.

She leaned further, straining to see. Her shadow seemed to split. Something bright broke the surface of the water, vanished for an instant, and broke, glimmering again.

'Dolphin!' cried a voice.

Stella turned, surprised to see that others had found her corner of the boat. Three young men drinking cans of beer, their voices loud.

'There it is again! See?'

It really was a dolphin. Stella hadn't recognised it straightaway because it had been keeping pace with the boat right in the spot where her shadow fell across the water. That was why her shadow had seemed so alive.

As she watched, a second dolphin rose close by. She saw the arch of its back and the pale, speeding arrow of its head, just below the surface.

'You ever seen dolphins here before?' one of the men asked. 'I've never seen them here before.'

They crowded beside her at the rail, staring and pointing. She shrank back, suddenly remembering that she'd taken off her cap for fear of losing it in the wind. She shoved it on and made her way to the other side of the boat. In the safety of the cramped ferry bathroom, she tucked the last few strands of her hair under the cap and stared at herself in the mirror. With her shorts and T-shirt and plain grey jacket, she could pass for a boy. The only thing that might give her away was her necklace.

She hesitated. Then she unclasped the chain and pushed the necklace deep into the pocket of her shorts, where it couldn't fall out.

They were clear of the bay now. The sun had burned away the last of the haze, and light broke in a million points across the lively water. The sea darkened to a rich blue and became choppy. A golden smudge appeared in the distance, growing clearer as the ferry approached. A long line of dunes, empty as the desert.

Lastland Island looked as remote as Stella had imagined.

Then the ferry made a turn around the line of dunes, and she realised how wrong she'd been.

Seventeen

They were entering a wide, curving harbour, lined with buildings, and even from this distance, Stella could see it was bustling with life. Umbrellas dotted the beach, flags flew along the pier, and the dock was crowded with vessels of all shapes and sizes.

Stella followed the passengers off the boat. She walked down the pier, past vendors selling ice cream and streamers and seaside souvenirs, and stopped at the end, under a sign with a giant lobster so red that it hurt her eyes. Beyond lay the main street, its pavements packed tight with people. Stella slipped into the throng, too dazed to worry if anyone might recognise her.

Nobody gave her a second glance. There were too many other things to steal their attention. Bunting fluttered, music blared from every storefront, performers in feathers and sequins paraded, and restaurants spilled on to the pavement, the chatter of diners and the chink of cutlery adding to the hubbub.

A young man in a top hat was handing out fliers on a corner. Stella plucked up her courage and approached him.

'Do you know a place called Crystal Cove? I think it might be a beach, or maybe a bay...'

He shook his head, already looking away.

She crossed the road, narrowly dodging a trio of bicycles weaving along in the opposite direction and entered a busy coffee shop.

'What can I get you?'

'I'm looking for Crystal Cove.'

'Does she work here?'

'It's not a person, it's a place,' Stella told the woman behind the bar, but the clank and hiss of the coffee machine drowned her words.

She carried on down the main street, the sun hot on the back of her neck, her legs tired. She was nearly at the end of the long strip of shops and restaurants before she dared ask for directions again. An old man with a stick was coming towards her, walking so slowly that she felt sure he wouldn't mind stopping for a moment or two.

'Can you tell me the way to Crystal Cove?'

He peered at her in silence, leaning on his stick and wheezing, as if the sheer effort of thinking was using up the last of his energy.

'Not sure if it's still there,' he said finally. 'Perhaps...'

He pointed in the direction Stella had come. 'All the way down, right at the end. You'll have to hunt for it.'

Stella retraced her steps and was halfway down the fourth side street, when she saw it. Not a beach or a bay, but another shop, although there didn't seem to be anything for sale in the window. Perhaps some kind of office, then, Stella thought. The name was written in blue above the window, with the first letters of 'Crystal' and 'Cove' made to look like white-tipped, cresting waves. Propped up against the inside of the window was a large photograph. Stella could see it clearly from the other side of the street.

It showed two mermaids, swimming towards the surface of a light-filled ocean, in a cloud of bubbles as bright as stars.

Stella crossed the road, her heart thumping with excitement, although as she came nearer, she couldn't help noticing how shabby the place seemed. The window was grubby and smeared, and the photograph was askew, its edges yellowed from exposure to sunlight. She squinted at the sign. There were words in smaller letters running below the name.

East of the Dee and West of the Wave!

Stella could tell it was meant to say 'Deep' because the shadow of the 'p' was still there. It had obviously fallen off some time ago, and never been replaced. She shielded her eyes and peered through the glass.

There was a desk — or a counter of some kind — and the shape of a woman behind it. Stella drew back at once, but the woman lifted her hand, beckoning, as if she had been watching Stella through the glass, waiting to catch her eye.

Stella hesitated, caught by a feeling of unease. She had come too far to turn back now, though. She took a deep breath and pushed open the door.

The room smelled of chlorine, and the sharp-sweet tang of artificial pine. A pink plaster seahorse stood at one end of the counter, a garish clam at the other, with the woman sitting in between.

'Welcome!' she said in a bright voice. 'Please come in!'

Stella was too bewildered to reply.

'You're just in time!'

Perhaps the woman had mistaken her for someone else. She was solid-looking, with dark grey hair cut short, and a wide, rosy, weather-beaten face.

'We're just about to start,' the woman said. 'You're in luck, there are still a couple of seats left.'

'Seats?' Stella echoed. She looked around and saw a door with the words 'VIEWING GALLERY' written above, and frayed rope barriers on either side. 'Oh!' she said, turning automatically towards the gallery door. 'Oh, I see.'

'You'll have to pay for a ticket,' the woman said, her voice suddenly sharp.

Stella's face grew hot with embarrassment. She rummaged in her pocket for the last of her money.

'I don't have enough.'

The woman pursed her lips, and Stella turned to leave.

'Maybe we can make an exception,' the woman said. 'How much d'you have?'

She took the money and placed it in the till. Stella noticed a plastic tub with a picture of a dead fish taped to the side, and the words, *Please! Help Save Our Seas!* written in black marker around the top.

The woman waved her hand, not looking at Stella. 'You can go through.'

A heavy, dull-coloured curtain hung at the entrance to the viewing gallery. Stella drew it back and stepped inside.

Eighteen

She was standing at the top of a ramp leading into near darkness, thick with the smell of lingering damp. Stella descended, her eyes adjusting to the dim light, and found herself in an auditorium with five or six rows of wooden benches facing faded velvet curtains.

The woman at the front desk had said there were only a couple of seats left. In fact, the place was practically deserted, apart from an elderly couple at the back, a woman with a wriggling child on her lap, and a ragged-looking man who appeared to be asleep.

Stella had no sooner sat down before she heard a crackle of static, and a booming voice.

'Come, come with me, all seekers of adventure, to a land of mystery, east of the deep and west of the wave…'

The curtains gave a whining creak and began to open in a jerky fashion.

'Here, in a cavern strewn with pearls, live the people of the sea…'

Stella found herself staring into a tank, at least six metres tall and twice as wide. The glass was cloudy, stained green with creeping algae. On the left side, piled on top of each other, three boulders formed a tower. A greyish plastic coral stood on the right. The sandy bottom was scattered with white globes, which Stella assumed were meant to be the 'pearls', although they looked suspiciously like ping-pong balls.

'These are the immortals, never growing old, never dying, beautiful forever.'

A light came on in the back of the tank, turning the plastic coral a sickly pink. Bubbles drifted up from behind the rocky tower, something swam into view, and Stella suddenly understood everything.

The girl had sequins sewn on to her bikini top, and a long purple tail, and a smile that appeared as fixed to her face as the shells glued to her long black hair.

She was dressed up to look like a mermaid. It was a *show*.

Thoughts tumbled through Stella's mind, falling into place one after the other. Her mum must have worked here, as a performer. Perhaps the girl in the drawing had been a performer too.

So *that* was what Gramma had meant!

The girl in the tank reached the front and waved stiffly.

Stella couldn't move, overcome by her own stupidity. Her mum hadn't been a *real* mermaid! There was no such thing! How could Stella have believed — even for a minute — that there was?

'Few travellers ever catch sight of these sirens of the deep,' droned the voice, 'for they are shy creatures.'

The girl reached down with an awkward thrust of her tail, picked up a ping-pong ball, and pretended to admire it.

'This is boring!' the child in the audience cried loudly. 'Bor-ring!'

Maybe she'd only *half*-believed it, Stella told herself. Her eyes roamed over the algae-encrusted tank, and the fake coral.

Maybe not even half.

In the water, the girl's smile was strained. Stella wondered how much longer she could hold her breath.

How Cam had laughed at Stella! As if it was a big joke. Well, maybe it had been, Stella thought. Maybe she had been joking all along, without really knowing.

The more she considered it, the more likely this seemed, and by the time the show came to an end, in a burst of music and a wild flickering of lights, she'd convinced herself.

She'd definitely been joking. She'd never believed it.

The elderly couple and the mother and child were already making their way to the exit. Even the ragged man seemed to be stirring, roused from his sleep by the noise. Stella stood up, feeling almost light-hearted.

Her lovely mum had been a regular, normal human being. And Stella wasn't strange, or different in any way. Not weird-weird, she thought, smiling to herself. Just weird-*interesting*.

The woman in the front office was shaking the *Save Our Seas!* donation tub in the direction of the elderly couple. They deposited a few coins and hurried off. Stella approached the counter. It didn't matter now if she was recognised. She was going home anyway.

'Excuse me.'

The woman was peering into the donation tub, stirring the coins as if counting them. How large her hands were. The kind of hands that were good at working heavy machinery. Or wielding an axe.

Stella didn't know why that last thought had come into her head. She smiled politely.

'I think my mum used to work here,' she said shyly. 'It was a long time ago. I just wondered whether you remember her.'

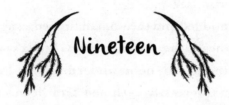

Nineteen

'That's nice,' the woman said, still stirring the coins. 'What's her name?'

Stella told her, and the woman looked up at once, the donation tub poised mid-air, as if she had forgotten she was holding it.

'Is she here? Is she with you?'

Stella shook her head. 'I'm on my own. She's—'

'Take off your cap,' the woman ordered. 'Let's have a look at you.'

'I don't look anything like Mum...' Stella said. The woman took a step forward, staring intently. She was so close Stella could see the web of broken red veins in her cheeks, and the glitter of excitement in her dark eyes.

'Would you do me a favour?' the woman asked. 'Could you stay here, just for a moment? There's someone who would love to meet you.'

'I guess so.'

'You promise?'

Stella nodded and the woman turned away, towards the entrance to the viewing gallery. Stella saw that she was wearing cowboy boots underneath her long skirt. The boots were silver-tipped and decorated with spurs at the heel that made a sharp, jangling noise with every step. In the doorway, the woman looked back.

'You promise now?' she repeated.

'Yes,' Stella said. 'I promise.'

A door slammed, and a moment later the woman reappeared, pushing a girl in a rusty-looking wheelchair.

'What do you think?' she asked. 'She look like Aquabelle to you?'

Stella was confused. 'That's not my mum's name.'

'Of course not,' the woman said. She gestured towards the wheelchair. 'This is Pearl. That's not her real name either.'

Up close, Stella could see that Pearl was a good deal

older than she first seemed, although her face was as smooth as a girl's. But her skin lacked colour, and her hair was thin and wispy. Even her shabby dress, faded to a greenish memory, looked washed out. As if she had been painted entirely in watercolours.

'I'm forgetting my manners,' the woman said. 'I haven't introduced myself. I'm Marcie. And you are?'

'Stella.'

'What a pretty name!' Marcie said. 'Isn't that a pretty name, Pearl?'

Pearl stared at Stella, her face expressionless. There was something familiar about her, although Stella couldn't put her finger on what it was.

'Your mother,' Pearl said, her voice hesitant. 'Where is she?'

'She's... she's not here,' Stella stammered. 'I mean, she's dead. She died when I was eight.'

A ripple passed over Pearl's face. Her clasped hands tightened. Then, as slowly as a leaf drifting from a tree, her gaze fell to her lap.

'Dead!' Marcie cried. 'Oh, that's awful!'

The news had really upset them, Stella thought. They must have liked her mum a lot.

'I'm sorry,' she said.

Marcie shook her head. 'What a loss,' she muttered. 'Such a star...'

'So she *did* work here.'

'Of course she did! Pearl performed with her. They were... best friends. Isn't that right, Pearl?'

Marcie jiggled the handles of the wheelchair and Pearl nodded.

'We should show Stella the pictures,' Marcie said. 'Don't you think, Pearl?

I bet you'd like to see some pictures of your mother,' she said to Stella. 'We could have some tea. Are you hungry?'

'I guess so,' Stella said, although in fact she was almost dizzy with hunger. The bar of chocolate and handful of biscuits that she'd eaten on the dock felt like a long time ago. And it was also true that she would love to see pictures of her mum and listen to stories about her life before Stella had even been born. It would make her mum feel real to Stella again, still alive, if only in memory.

Nevertheless, she hesitated. The gloomy interior of the Crystal Cove seemed smaller than before, as if the walls were closing in on her, and there was something unsettling about the two women, particularly Pearl.

The way she sat, unsmiling, her face so very pale…

Stella peered outside. It was growing dark. 'I don't know,' she said. 'I ought to be getting back.'

'What a shame,' Marcie said. 'After such sad news, it would have been good to talk about old times.' She looked so disappointed that Stella felt ashamed.

'Well, okay,' she said. 'I'll stay for a little bit longer.'

Twenty

Stella followed Marcie and Pearl back into the viewing gallery. Marcie turned the light on, although it was still extremely dim, little more than a yellow filter over the dark. Stella saw — with a feeling of relief — that the curtains remained lowered, hiding the tank. She heard the sound of water gurgling through pipes.

'Don't mind the noise,' Marcie called over her shoulder. 'We drain the tank every other week so we can give it a good clean.'

Marcie pushed the wheelchair to the bottom of the ramp and turned right, crossing the front of the gallery. She pointed to a pair of shadowy doors.

'Through there's the entrance to the tank, plus dressing rooms. It's where we keep all our costumes and props.' She smiled at Stella. 'It's where the magic happens!'

Stella nodded politely, thinking of the ping-pong balls, and the sequins missing from the mermaid's tail.

'And this is where we call home,' Marcie announced, stopping by a door on the far side of the gallery. She held it open, and Pearl wheeled herself through, navigating with strong, deft movements.

The room was brighter than the viewing gallery, but with the same yellowish tint. There was a stretch of countertop on one side, with a microwave, stove and five or six chipped wooden cabinets. On the other side a desk piled with papers in messy heaps around an ancient-looking computer. There was something odd about the place, although it was a while before Stella realised what it was. The room had no windows.

Marcie gestured to the wall above the desk. It was covered with hundreds of photographs, fliers and old newspaper cuttings.

'My wall of memories,' she said.

Stella stepped forward eagerly.

'There she is,' Marcie said, tapping one of the photos. 'Aquabelle!'

Stella saw a group of five young women in shiny skirts and matching bikini tops. They were standing in a row, the sleek, curling waves of their hair spilling over their shoulders. Stella's mum was in the middle.

Her eyelids glittered behind long black lashes, and her lips were painted the kind of red that only the most beautiful – or the most daring – can ever wear. Stella caught her breath, transfixed by a feeling in which joy lay so close to sadness that it was impossible to tell where one began and the other ended.

Marcie tapped another photo. 'That's her in the tank.'

Stella knew her mum had been good at swimming, but she hadn't known quite how good. The picture showed her and another woman – both wearing mermaid tails – floating effortlessly under the water. Their backs were arched, and their bodies formed identical C shapes.

'CC,' Marcie explained. 'For "Crystal Cove". Only two girls have ever been able to perfect that formation. Your mother and Pearl.'

Stella darted a look at the wheelchair.

'I know,' Marcie said, catching the look. 'Hard to believe, isn't it?'

Stella decided she didn't like Marcie, although Pearl didn't seem to have heard the hurtful comment. She sat still, her face vacant, her hands in her lap.

'That was the heyday of the Crystal Cove, when your mother worked here,' Marcie said, her hands travelling slowly over the pictures. 'Those were the glory days.'

Stella saw another image of her mum, dressed casually this time, her arm around a much younger Marcie. They were standing in the viewing gallery. The place looked completely different. Chandeliers hung from the ceiling, and rich red carpet covered the floor.

'We had five shows a day back then,' Marcie said, a dreamy expression crossing her face. 'Six at the weekend. Every show was packed. The public would form a queue all the way down the street.'

'What happened?' Stella asked.

'I guess you could say we lost... the magic,' Marcie said, giving Pearl a sidelong glance. 'How about that tea?' she added sharply.

Pearl wheeled around automatically, and began filling the kettle and gathering mugs. Stella noticed she used a tool to get to items that were beyond the reach of her wheelchair. It was a makeshift thing, a broken-off broom handle with a coat hook attached to one end.

'Pearl's very handy with that little stick of hers,' Marcie told Stella. 'She gets through the chores in no time.'

'Sit,' she added, pulling a chair from under the kitchen table.

The top of the table was grey plastic, scratched and slightly sticky to the touch. Stella kept her hands on her lap, waiting for the tea. Marcie began to talk about the mermaid costumes, how Stella's mum had had five tails in different colours. They had been made especially for her and fitted so well it was impossible to see the join.

'No need for a wig, of course,' Marcie said. 'Not with that magnificent hair of hers.'

Pearl put two cups of tea on the table, and Stella took a sip. It tasted bad, the milk slightly sour.

'Don't you like tea?' Marcie said. 'Drink it!'

Stella took another mouthful. She glanced at

the closed door on the opposite side of the room, wondering where it led. To more windowless rooms, perhaps? She wiped her mouth, feeling nauseous.

'No doubt about it, Aquabelle was special,' Marcie was saying. 'Everyone could see it, although none of the other girls were jealous because Aquabelle never bragged, she was always so nice.

She was a sweetheart,' Marcie said. 'Isn't that right, Pearl?'

Pearl nodded silently, her eyes fixed on the empty space in the middle of the table.

'Where did you meet?' Stella asked Pearl. 'You said she was your best friend.'

'We grew up together.'

Stella frowned slightly. Her mum had never mentioned having a best friend.

'What do you mean?' she asked. But Pearl said nothing more.

'Oh, don't pay any attention to Miss Misery!' Marcie cried. 'We have so much more to talk about.'

The edges of the room had grown blurry and the white oval of Pearl's face gleamed like the inside of a shell.

'We were wondering whether you were like your

mother,' Marcie said.

'I don't understand.'

'In the water, I mean,' Marcie said.

Stella shook her head, although the movement made her dizzy. 'No,' she said. 'I can swim but I haven't...' She wanted to finish the sentence, but there was a buzzing in her ears that made it hard to think.

She fumbled for the bag at her feet and stood up. 'I have to go,' she said. 'I have to, but thank you for the tea it wasveryniceofyou...'

'You don't look well, are you okay?' Marcie said.

The room tilted. 'I'm fine,' Stella said. 'I'm—'

She was half-lying, half-sitting on the floor, without a clear idea of how she'd got there. She felt Marcie's hand grasp her arm.

'She needs to lie down. Get the door for me.'

'No, I don't want to, I want to go home,' Stella said, although the words got stuck before they could come out.

She was walking — or rather being walked — down a narrow corridor, the ceiling low and dark, Marcie solid as the side of a cliff beside her. Then they were in another room with two beds, and Stella was sitting down, closing her eyes.

When she opened them, Pearl was leaning over her, pressing a glass of water to her lips. Stella took a sip, and then another. Pearl's eyes were a peculiar colour, turquoise rather than blue, as clear and as pure as the rims on Gramma's teacups back at home.

'You fainted, nothing to make a fuss about,' Marcie said. She rested her weight against the door, and Stella heard the click as it closed. 'You need to eat.'

Pearl pushed something into Stella's hand. It was a sandwich, the bread as pale as the plate it was resting on. Stella shook her head.

'I'm fine, it's okay.'

'*Eat it*,' Marcie snapped.

Pearl laid a cool, feathery hand on her arm, and Stella felt a stab of fear.

'Best do as she says,' Pearl whispered.

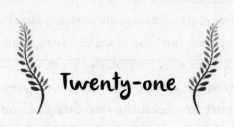

Twenty-one

If there was any flavour in the sandwich's thin slice of ham, Stella was incapable of tasting it. She chewed as best she could, praying she would be able to swallow the food, and keep it down.

Marcie stepped away from the door. 'Feeling better?'

Stella nodded, still chewing. She did feel better; all she had needed was to eat.

'I'm okay now,' she said. 'I'm fine, but I have to go. I don't want to miss the last ferry.' She would have liked to get up, but Marcie was close to the bed, towering over her.

'I don't think so,' she said.

Stella was too shocked to move for a second. Then she leaped up and made a dash for the door.

It was locked.

'Open it! Let me go!'

Pearl gasped. 'Marcie, you said you wouldn't…'

'You can't stop me from leaving,' Stella interrupted. 'That's… that's kidnap. That's a *crime*.'

'Yes, it is,' Marcie agreed. 'So it's lucky nobody knows you're here, isn't it, Stella *Martin*?'

Stella couldn't speak.

'I follow the news, you know,' Marcie said. 'I'm not a dummy. You're a runaway, and everyone is looking for you. But I bet they won't be looking for you here.'

'Why are you doing this?' Stella whispered.

'I just want to ask you some questions. Sit back down.'

The woman was mad, Stella thought, returning to the bed. She had to stay calm, pretend to play along.

'How did you know to come here?' Marcie demanded. 'What did your mother tell you?'

Stella shook her head. 'Nothing… I worked it out.'

'Seems I'll have to fill you in, then.'

'Marcie, *don't*,' Pearl whimpered from the corner.

'Where should I begin?' Marcie said.

'Please, Marcie, *please*,' Pearl begged, wringing her hands until the knuckles shone white.

Marcie eyed her impatiently. 'Go and do the washing up, Pearl.'

The woman in the wheelchair hesitated. Stella watched as she turned, wheeled slowly across the room, and began to manoeuvre her chair through the door.

It would be easy to push past her. What could Pearl do to stop her escaping? But Marcie was there, between Stella and the door, and Stella knew there was no pushing past *her*.

Marcie paced to and fro, the spurs on her cowboy boots jangling.

'I'd been running the Crystal Cove for almost three years when your mother turned up,' she began. 'The show was a lot better in those days. I had more girls, the costumes were new, and we were still a novelty in town. But at heart, it was the same as it is now. A piece of make-believe. An act.'

Stella didn't know why Marcie was telling her this. There was a strange look on her face, the same one she'd worn earlier, when showing Stella the old photographs. As if she was reliving some wonderful dream.

'Then your mother came, and the show took off,' Marcie continued. 'It became a sensation. There was a simple reason for that, although I didn't know what it was for a long time.'

Marcie stopped pacing. The room was silent. Stella knew that not far off, there were shops and restaurants and noisy streets thronged with holidaymakers, music and laughter and friendly faces. But in the dim, windowless depths of the Crystal Cove, they might just as well have been a thousand miles away.

'Then one day, I discovered the truth,' Marcie said.

'I don't know what you're talking about!' Stella cried.

Marcie bent in close, her mottled cheeks quivering. 'Your mother was a performer like all the other girls. She was putting on an act. But what, might you ask, was she pretending?'

'I don't know,' Stella said, leaning desperately away from Marcie's looming face. 'How should I know?'

Marcie smiled in triumph. 'She was pretending to pretend!'

Stella stared at her blankly.

'Okay,' Marcie said, straightening up and beginning to pace again. 'Let me put it another way.

Did you ever have bath toys when you were a little kid? Did you ever have one of those wind-up plastic fish?

You turn the cog, and put it in the water,' she continued, without waiting for Stella to answer. 'The little tail jerks back and forth, and it moves like it's swimming. You've seen toys like that, haven't you?'

'I… I guess so.'

'Of course you have. They look like fish, and they move like fish, *sort of*. Until their cog runs down and you have to wind them up again. But if you were to put a real fish in your bathtub, you'd realise how lame the plastic one truly was. Nothing like the real thing. Just a silly fake.'

Stella's mouth had gone dry, and when she tried to swallow, it felt as though there was something hard and scratchy lodged in the top of her throat.

'Do you see where I'm going with this?' Marcie said. 'It's a — what do you call it? — a metaphor. The bathtub is like our tank here at the Crystal Cove, and the girls who perform in it are like the plastic fish, except that instead of a cog that needs to be wound up, they have to come up for air every few minutes. But your mother…'

Marcie's voice had risen. Her eyes locked on to Stella's face.

'Your mother was the real fish!'

Stella sat pinned, unable to move or speak. 'That's right,' Marcie said. 'An actual, real-as-you-or-me, mermaid.' She tapped the side of her head with her forefinger. 'And I was the one who discovered her!'

It wasn't true, it couldn't be, she'd never even half-believed it. It had only been a joke...

'You're mad!' Stella burst out. 'You're mad, let me go!' And she covered her ears with her hands.

'Am I?' Marcie said. 'Well, if you don't believe me, ask Pearl. She's one too.' She crossed to the door, her boots thumping on the bare floorboards. 'It's late,' she said. 'You'll think differently in the morning.'

Stella heard the click as the door swung to and locked.

Twenty-two

Stella lay curled up, too tired to think straight, and too frightened to sleep. Apart from the two beds, the only other furniture in the room was a wardrobe with a full-length mirror, speckled with age. There was nothing inside except a solitary coat hanger that rattled when she opened the door. The bed she lay on was made up, although it was hard to imagine anyone having a good night's sleep between the musty sheets.

Stella stared at the bare light bulb, and the shadows running across the damp-stained ceiling. Marcie had said it was late, although Stella had no idea what time it really was, or whether she would even know when the morning came. Without windows, there was no way to tell whether it was dark or light outside. Hours and hours could pass without her knowing. What if she lost track of time completely, Stella thought, and whole *days* went by?

Then she remembered she was wearing her watch. In the empty room, its green glow was a tiny beacon of reassurance.

Nearly midnight. Stella thought about turning off the light — the switch was next to the door. But darkness was a frightening prospect. In that little room, it would be a darkness to make her lose all bearings, so that even if she changed her mind and wanted to turn the light back on, she couldn't, because she'd no longer have any idea where the switch was...

Stella shivered. She pulled the thin blanket off the bed, and wrapped it tightly around her. Her hand went to her throat feeling for her necklace.

It wasn't there.

She felt a flare of intense, sickening panic. Then she remembered she'd taken off the necklace on the ferry. It was still in the pocket of her shorts. She patted the fabric, feeling the familiar shape of the stone.

Home had never felt so distant. Stella felt a rush of longing for everything she had left behind. For her dad, and for Gramma, and Mrs Chapman, and even for Tina. They would all be looking for her, although Marcie was right; they wouldn't be looking for her here. She was too far away.

But Cam wasn't.

Stella sat up a little straighter. Cam and her family would have reached their new home by now. The thought that Cam was not far away on the mainland made Stella clench her fists with frustration. If only she'd waited until Cam had arrived, if only she'd told her where she was going...

If only they hadn't argued. But hadn't she told Cam she'd go to Lastland Island some day? She'd spoken so angrily, surely Cam would remember. Would she think of it now, and guess where Stella was?

Maybe, Stella thought, although she couldn't count on it. Even for Cam it wasn't much to go on. Her heart – which had briefly lifted in hope – sank back down again. Her eyes wandered hopelessly around the dreary room. There was a mark on the headboard of her bed, right in the corner. Stella leaned in for a better look.

She gasped. It was a picture of a turtle, scratched in the wood.

Stella knew her mum had made it. She'd recognise her style anywhere. She reached out and touched the picture with the tip of her finger, and a surge of love and comfort washed over her. It was so strong and so real that it was almost as if Stella's mum herself had entered the room, and taken her into her arms.

The turtle was about six centimetres high, viewed from below, showing the animal's belly and the underside of its head, with its flippers spread on either side. It had been drawn with nothing more than a needle, yet it was so lifelike and complete. Stella could see the markings on its belly, all the lines in its leathery neck and flippers. Her mum must have made it when she lived at the Crystal Cove, years and years ago. It had been on the headboard all this time, waiting for Stella like a message of hope and reassurance.

I haven't left you, the message seemed to say. *I am here with you now. Be strong…*

Stella lay down, her hand resting against the headboard, as close to the picture of the turtle as she could get. She closed her eyes. Her last thought before falling asleep was of Cam, so near across the water.

She didn't know whether Cam had remembered their talk about Lastland Island or not. But Stella suddenly thought of a way she might be able to remind her.

Twenty-three

Stella woke early to the sound of the door opening. She leaped to her feet, instantly awake. Pearl wheeled through the door, closing it behind her with a quick flip of her makeshift hook. She was wearing a slightly less dingy dress, and her hair was scraped into a bun, although her efforts only made her seem more pitiful. As she crossed the room, she looked as insubstantial as her own cloudy reflection, flickering in the wardrobe mirror.

'I brought you breakfast,' she said. A cup of tea and a piece of toast — the butter spread extremely thin — lay on a tray on her lap. She placed the tray on the bed next to Stella.

'I don't want it,' Stella said. 'I want to go home.'

'I'm sorry,' Pearl said, her eyes downcast.

Stella had the feeling that Pearl didn't like what Marcie was doing any more than Stella did.

'If you're sorry, why don't you let me out?'

'Even if I let you through the door, it wouldn't be any good,' Pearl said. 'You have to go through the kitchen to get to the front, and Marcie's there, like, always. She sleeps next to the desk, on a pull-out cot.'

'You could call someone.'

'She's got the only phone.'

'You could go out yourself, then!' Stella cried. 'You could get help, tell the police...'

Pearl twisted her pale hands together. 'I can't,' she said, her voice anguished. 'I daren't, you don't understand.'

'You're frightened of her,' Stella said.

Pearl's lips tightened until her mouth almost vanished. 'She's a terrible person,' she said with sudden feeling. 'Cruel and stupid and reckless.'

'She's mad,' Stella said.

'Yes. But not in the way you think.'

'Why do you stay here if you hate her so much?'

'I more than hate her,' Pearl said. 'There isn't a

word for how I feel.' She broke off, shaking her head. 'I'm sorry about your mother. More sorry than you can know.'

She looked up, and Stella saw that her eyes were red-rimmed, and her face had a raw, rubbed look, as if she had been crying for a long time, through the night.

'Not an hour has gone by in all these years that I haven't thought about her,' Pearl said. 'I wonder, did she ever... say anything about me?'

Stella shook her head.

'No,' Pearl said in a low voice. 'Of course not, how could she?'

Again she paused. 'Tell me,' she said at last. 'Was she happy?'

It was a strange question. Stella had never thought of it quite like that before. The memory of a long-ago summer night came back to her. She had been in bed, and had come downstairs, although she didn't know why. She remembered stopping at the foot of the stairs. The windows were open, letting in the night air, and she could hear music playing. Her parents were dancing together in the living room, under a circle of light. It was old-fashioned dancing, the kind with proper steps. But Stella could tell her mum wasn't quite sure of them, because she kept glancing at her feet, and trying not to laugh. And every time she did, Stella's dad's smile grew wider, and he held her closer, and their shadows flowed over the walls of the living room. Stella thought they might have stayed dancing like that for ever, if they hadn't seen her standing there.

She gazed at Pearl, her mind bright with the memory.

'I think she was the happiest person in the whole world,' Stella said.

Pearl sighed, as if a weight had been lifted off her. 'I'm glad,' she said. 'So it was worth it...'

'What do you mean?'

Pearl looked away without answering.

Stella had been sitting on the edge of the bed, but now she pushed her body back against the wall, and drew up her knees protectively. Pearl wasn't to be trusted, any more than Marcie.

'I thought you were on my side,' she said. 'But you're on hers. You're going to say the same crazy thing she did. That you and my mum were actual—' Stella broke off, unable to finish the sentence.

'It's not crazy,' Pearl said, her voice calm, and sad.

Stella had run away from home because she thought her mum might have been a mermaid. Sometimes it's easy to believe something — however unlikely — when it is just a vague theory. But the more real it gets, the harder it becomes, and now all Stella's common sense rose in rebellion.

'There are no such things as mermaids!' she burst out. 'Mum told me that herself!'

'She was right.'

Stella stared at her in confusion.

'There's no such thing, if you mean those creatures who sit on rocks and comb their hair all day,' Pearl said, with a hint of scorn. 'The ones with pretty tails, who sing to ships, or change into seals, or lure sailors to their doom for no apparent reason. There's no such thing as *them*.'

'What, then?'

'Imagine what you would need to live in the deepest, wildest ocean,' Pearl said. 'The eel's whip and the limpet's cling, the strength and sleepless eyes of the great white shark, the liquid shiver of the squid... like *that*.

Most people would be frightened if they saw it,' she added. 'Even horrified.'

'That's impossible!' Stella protested. 'It doesn't—'

She was interrupted by a familiar jingling noise. The door swung open and Marcie walked in. She was wearing jeans tucked into the top of her boots, and they gave her legs a stumpy look, as shapeless as a pair of tree trunks. She gazed at Stella with a look of deep satisfaction.

'So how's our little guest this morning?'

Twenty-four

'Not going to talk to me?' Marcie grinned. 'That's not very polite. Perhaps you don't like your accommodation. Nothing like that big, fancy house of yours.

I did a little research,' she continued. 'Your father's a rich man.'

'He'll pay you,' Stella said. 'He'll pay you anything if you let me go.'

'Well, *probably*,' Marcie said with mean emphasis. 'But that would spoil everything.'

Stella was too distracted to work out what she meant. She was thinking about the plan she'd hatched the night before. If it had any chance, she would have to be careful. Very careful.

'It doesn't really matter if you ask my dad for money or not,' she said, trying to sound casual. 'The police will be here soon, anyway.'

'I don't think so,' Marcie said.

'I told my friend I was coming here,' Stella said. 'She's the only one who knows. She said if I didn't call her by nine o' clock this morning to say I was okay, she'd tell my dad where I was.'

She was talking too fast, Stella thought. She needed to sound more confident.

'Nice try,' Marcie said, although a hint of uncertainty had entered her voice.

'You should let me go now,' Stella said.

Marcie made a scoffing sound. 'Do you believe her, Pearl? I don't.'

Pearl shot Stella a frightened glance.

'I think she's making it up,' Marcie said. She strode to the bed and leaned over Stella.

'Do you think I'm a *dummy*?'

Stella's heart was beating so hard she felt sure Marcie could see it thumping beneath her jacket. She forced herself to look her in the eye.

'Her name is Camilla Jenkins,' she said. 'She lives in the town on the mainland, near the ferry.'

Marcie's eyes narrowed.

'It's nearly nine o'clock,' Stella said.

'I can tell the time, thank you very much!' Marcie spat.

'Maybe you should let her go...' Pearl ventured timidly.

A look of indecision crossed Marcie's face. Then she straightened up.

'No!' She pulled a phone from the back pocket of her jeans.

'Call her,' she told Stella. 'Call her now. Tell her you're just fine.'

Stella was so surprised at the success of her plan that she almost took the phone from Marcie's hand. But it would look suspicious if she was too eager. She was supposed to be *hoping* that Cam would call the police.

'I'm not calling,' she said. 'You can't make me.'

Marcie sat next to her, the bed shifting under her weight.

'Tell me her number.'

'I don't know it,' Stella said. 'I can't remember.'

'If you don't tell me,' Marcie said, almost kindly, 'you'll never get out of here. You'll never go home. That's a promise.'

Stella believed her.

'You'll tell her you met a couple of your mother's friends,' Marcie said. 'Keep it short, no chatting. And don't even think about trying anything.'

Stella nodded, her throat tight with fear.

'I'll know if you try anything,' Marcie said.

Stella watched as she tapped the numbers, and then Marcie handed her the phone.

'Hi, Cam,' Stella croaked.

'Stella!' Cam's familiar voice was a shriek in her ear. 'Wh—'

'I got to Lastland Island, like I told you I would,' Stella said, cutting her off. 'Only you can't tell anyone, you have to promise.'

She pressed the phone tightly to her ear, so that Marcie couldn't hear Cam's squawks of amazement.

'Everyone's looking for you!' Cam exclaimed.

'I know,' Stella said. Marcie seized her arm in a threatening grip. 'I'm fine,' she said. 'Everything's fine. I've met some friends of my mum's…'

'You sure?'

Marcie's grip tightened until Stella winced.

'Yes,' she said. 'But you can't tell. Promise?'

Cam made more squawking sounds. 'Okay,' she

said at last. 'Call me soon, though, let me know…'

Marcie was gesturing for Stella to finish, half-reaching for the phone. In a few seconds Stella would have to hang up. But all she'd done was tell Cam where she was. She hadn't been able to tell her she was in danger.

'I know you think I'm weird,' she said in desperation. It was their private joke. Surely Cam would pick up on it.

'That's because you *are* weird,' Cam said.

Stella knew Cam would be expecting her to say, 'I know I am.'

'I am *not!*' she cried. 'I'm never weird. You're the weird one, not me!' She hung up before Cam had a chance to reply.

As a clue, it wasn't much to go on, but she hoped it would work.

'That wasn't so hard, was it?' Marcie said, tucking the phone into her pocket. 'Now we can get back to business.'

The look of satisfaction had returned to her face.

'We need to talk a little more about you and your mother.'

'I don't want to talk about my mum any more.

I don't believe anything you said about her. Or what *she* said,' she added, scowling at Pearl.

Marcie shrugged.

'You don't need to believe me, because it's true,' she said. 'I have proof.'

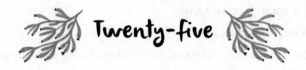

Twenty-five

'Go and fetch it, Pearl,' Marcie said. 'You know where it is.'

'You mustn't, you don't need to—' Pearl protested.

'Do as you're told.'

What proof could there possibly be? Stella strained her ears for any sounds from the outside. The police were on their way, she told herself.

'You'll understand,' Marcie was saying. 'This place was grand once, it was *grand*. But I never lost hope; I never gave up on my vision…'

Stella wasn't listening. She could hear the faint creak of the wheelchair getting louder and louder as Pearl made her way back. Then Pearl was in the room again. She had something on her lap. It was a moment before Stella realised what it was, because she had never seen one before.

It was a video camera. An old one, with a screen that folded out and a handle on the side, and a slot for a mini cassette tape.

Pearl handed it silently to Marcie.

Stella leaned forward without wanting to, gripped by a terrible curiosity. She couldn't take her eyes away as Marcie flipped open the little screen and ran her fingers over the buttons on the side of the camera, pressing to fast forward, stopping, then pressing again, her gaze fixed in concentration.

'Here's the place,' Marcie said. 'Yes, this is it.' She glanced at Stella. 'Come here. Look.'

Stella rose to her feet helplessly.

'It was shot from inside the tank,' Marcie said, holding out the camera so Stella could see the screen. 'That's the platform up above, where the performers enter.'

Stella saw a shifting, underwater view of rocks and plastic coral. Someone was sitting on the platform at the top, although she could only see part of a white bathrobe and a pair of bare, dangling legs.

'Your mother,' Marcie whispered harshly in her ear. 'See? Now she jumps in...'

The video cut. The tank was full of swirling bubbles. Stella glimpsed the flash of an arm, a kicking foot, a sudden drift of hair. Then the water cleared.

Her mum was facing away from the camera. Stella saw her shoulders and the top half of her back, her hair floating around her like a separate, living thing. She turned her head.

'Watch,' Marcie said, although Stella was hardly aware she had spoken.

Her mum's eyes were closed, and her face was perfectly still, so still that when her mouth parted, it was as if a statue had suddenly breathed. A great bubble of air rose from her lips, obscuring her face for a second. Her eyes opened.

'Watch!' Marcie repeated, even more urgently.

Stella frowned, blinking in the light of the tiny screen. Something was rising up her mum's back like a shadow, only far darker, and a hundred times more rich. She gleamed and seemed to flicker. Stella stared, her hand pressed hard against her mouth. Had her mum's eyes always been like that, so large, so impossibly bright, so—

'Stop it!' Pearl's voice was loud in the silent room. 'Leave her alone!'

On the screen, her mum's body glowed and shifted.

The strength and sleepless eyes of the great white shark, Stella thought. *The liquid shiver of the squid…*

She covered her face with her hands.

A moment passed, although it might have been an hour. Marcie and Pearl had gone, without Stella even noticing. She sat frozen on the bed.

It was true, all of it.

She hadn't needed to see the proof. In her heart she'd always known. She'd known by her necklace, with a stone so unusual that even the man at the Natural History Museum couldn't identify it. She'd known the minute she found the drawing hidden behind her mum's photograph. The turtle scratched on the headboard of this very bed had hinted at the truth. Only someone who had seen the underside of a turtle many, many times could have drawn it that way, so accurately, so full of detail.

Only someone used to looking at it from *below*.

But seeing the proof had made it official. Even Cam would have to believe it now. If only she could tell her, Stella thought, with a despairing glance at the locked door. Cam would never laugh at anything she said ever again.

Twenty-six

'I've brought you something to eat,' Pearl said.

Stella stared at the plastic tub of mac and cheese. It was already starting to congeal.

'I can't,' she said.

'You need your strength,' Pearl said. 'Your mum would have told you the same, wouldn't she?'

Stella wiped her eyes and nodded.

'Did she like to cook?' Pearl asked.

Stella nodded again. 'She wasn't very good. She always mixed funny things together to see what they would taste like.'

Pearl smiled. It was a real smile, the first Stella had seen, and for a moment, it transformed her face. 'Your mum was always inquisitive,' she said.

Stella looked at her uncertainly. 'When did she... when did you...?'

Pearl drew a deep breath as if gathering all her resolve. 'We came out of the sea,' she said at last, 'on the first day of summer, fourteen years ago.'

'But if you're not mermaids, who are you?' Stella asked. 'What are you called?'

'We're not called anything. We don't need language in the way you think of it. Names are no use to us. We are just... of the sea.'

'I don't understand. You say you came out of the water, but how did you know what to do? How did you know how to speak English?'

'We learn fast,' Pearl said. '*Really* fast.'

She shook her head, seeing the doubt on Stella's face. 'It always amazes me,' she said, 'the way humans think they're better than every other living thing.

They honestly believe they're the most intelligent, advanced creatures on the planet.'

She lifted her chin proudly as she spoke. Her meek expression had vanished, and it was possible to sense how she must have looked, years ago, when she was still full of strength. Stella caught her breath. There had been something familiar about Pearl when they first met, and now she knew what it was.

'How do you think we avoided detection all this time?' Pearl was saying. 'Even when the submarines and sonar came, the islands of plastic, the oil spills, the factory ships and the drag nets… do you think it was dumb *luck*?'

'I guess not,' Stella said, feeling ashamed.

'If you've always stayed hidden, why did you come up?'

'Because of your mother. She'd always been fascinated by the land. It was that terrible curiosity of hers. One day she made up her mind. I tried to talk her out of it, and I failed. I was never good at getting my own way, even then. The only thing I could do was come with her. She needed protection, you see. We stole two fisherman's coats from a boat out in the bay,' Pearl said, her eyes filling with memory. 'I can still see your mother's arm, whiter than wave's spray, reaching up to pull them from the boat railing. I can still hear her laughing.'

Twenty-seven

'We were lucky to arrive on the first day of summer. Lastland Island was celebrating with a grand parade. Among the flags and costumes and marching bands, nobody paid much attention to us in our fisherman's coats and bare feet. We walked down the main street, keeping close together, arms linked. But we couldn't have been feeling more different.

Right from the start, I could tell that our new environment entranced your mother. She had her head up, staring at everything with a look of wonder, as if any moment she might break into a skip of delight. I was filled with unease, though, all my instincts telling me that I didn't belong there.

I didn't like the
way I felt in my new skin.
The flat thud of my feet, the
dullness of my senses. Sounds
were muffled, and when I looked
around it was like peering at the world
through a tiny, dusty window. Even worse,
I'd lost connection to most of my body.
My heart was beating, blood ran through
my veins and nerves fired my muscles, but I
couldn't control any of it. I hardly even knew it was
happening. It was like existing inside a machine.

We passed a row of stalls selling food, and the
greasy smell of meat reached my nose, but apart from
that, the air was empty of information.

It was so different in the ocean!

I was so different.

You see, water carries traces of everything it
touches. Every shore and island, every pebble and
paddling foot, every life within it. And we of the sea
can read and understand it all, because our brains
aren't confined to a space inside our skulls. We can
think and feel with our entire bodies.

In the ocean, my fingertip could analyse the chemistry of a single drop of water, my bones judge the force of a wave, my ears calculate the cruising speed of a tanker, three horizons away. In the water, I'd been connected to a million lives and a million stories.

Here on Lastland Island, people appeared to drift along without much connection to anything. How could they live like that? So separate and unaware. Did they ever die from sheer loneliness?

My present body seemed a poor exchange for the one I'd had in the ocean. It wasn't only that I was physically far weaker, my spirit felt weaker too. I'd never been fearful before. Yet I was now. I stumbled along, tugging at your mother's arm.

If she shared any of my discomfort, she didn't show it. Her eyes ranged over the bunting hung across the street, the painted shop fronts, the crowds passing with their heavy shoes and sunburned faces. And she couldn't stop smiling.

I wasn't surprised. We of the sea have much of the human. We can take human form, after all. But your mother was born with far more than the rest of us. Already she was adapting to being on land.

A bulky, rosy-cheeked woman was handing out fliers on the corner of the street. She stared at us.

'Here for the summer?' she asked. 'Do you need work? I'm scouting for girls to perform in my show.'

She handed us one of the fliers. 'I'm looking for mermaids!'

We saw a picture of a woman with half of her body crammed into a fish-shaped bag and two shells stuck to her chest.

'How's your swimming?' the woman asked. We glanced at each other, smiling.

'Not… too bad,' your mother said.

'Foreigners, are you? Where's your luggage?'

We shrugged, not knowing what to say.

'I expect it was stolen,' the woman said. 'Foreigners are easy targets.' She gave us a sidelong look. 'I can't pay you much, you understand…'

She ushered us away, down a side street. We went with her, though I didn't like the way she looked at us.

As if we were things.

Things that she wanted.

'I'm Marcie,' she said, although she didn't ask our names, and wasn't curious about where we'd come from. The only thing that interested her was how well we might perform in the tank. When we told her we wouldn't get in unless we could wear long-sleeved tops as well as mermaid tails, she rolled her eyes in impatience. But her attitude changed once she saw us in the water. The tails slowed us down and it was hard not to laugh at the plastic coral and fake seaweed. Even so, after thirty seconds Marcie's mouth was agape.

'We'll call you Pearl and Aquabelle,' she announced, the instant we got out of the tank.

And, having no names ourselves, Pearl and Aquabelle we became, even to each other.

Marcie told us we could stay at the Crystal Cove, sharing a room for as long as we needed. I don't think she wanted to let us out of her sight. We began performing the next day. And from the start, we were a sensation.

NEW MERMAIDS 'MAKE WAVES' AT THE CRYSTAL COVE! ran the headline in the Lastland Gazette. Marcie read the article aloud, her voice gulping with excitement:

144 ⸖

'The Crystal Cove has become the hottest show in town with the arrival of newcomers, Pearl and Aquabelle. Their speed and grace leave the audience literally gasping with amazement. Apparently trained 'somewhere abroad', according to the Cove's owner, Marcie, the pair can stay submerged for astonishingly long periods of time. This reporter recorded nearly twelve minutes, without either performer showing any strain. Pearl and Aquabelle are clearly perfectly at home "under the sea"!'

It wasn't true. I didn't feel at home. Instead of growing used to my new life, I became more and more restless as the days passed. I hated my mermaid tail. It weighed me down and made my skin itch. I hated having to come up for air every few minutes, and the way the audience stared at me with their mouths hanging open as if I was a freak.

Most of all, I hated Marcie.

She fussed over us, bringing blankets for our beds and hot drinks at the slightest sign of a sniffle, buying us new clothes and showering us with flattery. But not long after we arrived, I glimpsed a different side to her.

The afternoon show had finished. I was still in the dressing room, and when I came out, I saw Marcie. She was kneeling on the platform, leaning out over the water. One of the performers was below. Marcie was shouting at her for not smiling enough during her routine.

'Happiness!' I heard her bellow. 'Joy!'

Suddenly her hands shot out and she pushed the girl's head underwater. She held her, flailing and thrashing, until she grinned in just the way Marcie wanted.

After that, I wasn't fooled by Marcie's sweet talk any more.

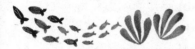

Twenty-eight

Every day my loathing of the Crystal Cove grew. But every day, Aquabelle seemed to enjoy it more. She made friends with the other girls. She wanted to know about their families, the towns they'd come from, their plans to travel the world, or start families of their own. She would sit for hours, sketching on a sandwich wrapper, asking endless questions.

She told me she longed to learn about art, and history, and the names of plants. How to ride a bike and drive a car.

I listened to her dreams with a sinking heart.

'Can't we stay just a few days longer?' she

would say whenever I spoke about returning. 'Just a couple of weeks…'

The queues of visitors to the Crystal Cove grew longer, and Marcie began to make serious money. She increased the ticket prices, and then increased them again. She bought flashy chandeliers and a new carpet for the viewing gallery, and talked about installing filming equipment to record the show.

The success of the Crystal Cove made her feel like a star.

One morning she appeared in a red satin jacket, and more fancy clothes quickly followed. Silk shirts, a white suit with mother of pearl buttons, a pair of cowboy boots with silver tips and spurs. She started going out every night.

Time passed. One night I saw a young man talking to Aquabelle. He'd seen the show and wanted to meet her. He was with an older woman, his mother. He came to the show again the following night, although this time he was by himself.

He was on holiday, Aquabelle told me. His name was Anthony. He knew about art *and* history.

When their holiday was over, his mother went home. But the young man stayed, and Aquabelle went out with him three nights in a row. The next week, they spent the whole of her day off together, and when she got back to the Crystal Cove, there was a light in her eyes I'd never seen before.

After that, she stopped saying, 'just a couple of weeks more,' or, 'a few days longer,' when I talked about returning.

She changed in other ways too. She grew distracted. One evening, during a performance, she forgot to pretend to come up for air, and drifted above the plastic coral, smiling to herself, until the audience grew uneasy, and then alarmed. What made it worse was that Marcie had installed the camera she'd been talking about, and was filming the entire show.

I had to pinch Aquabelle to remind her where she was. I pinched her harder than I needed to, out of jealousy as well as fear.

I've thought about that pinch many times. It wasn't such a terrible thing to do, yet I've always regretted it, because it was one of the last times I ever saw Aquabelle. Marcie found out our secret that very night.

Once again, it was forgetfulness that was to blame.

Twenty-nine

We'd formed the habit of slipping into the tank late in the evening, when the other girls had left and Marcie had gone out. With the Crystal Cove deserted, there was no need for our costumes. We could move with ease, relishing the feel of the water against our skin.

Aquabelle enjoyed it, but I *craved* it. It was the only time I was able to feel like myself again.

Swimming free like that, we were twice as fast, flickering from one side of the tank to the other in an instant. Mostly we rested, suspended in the water, as relaxed as if we were lounging in the park.

We were there as usual, the night I pinched Aquabelle to remind her to come up for air. She was happy; I could sense it through the water. It was a kind of total happiness, the sort that leaves no room for any other feeling, or any other person, except for one.

I sighed, my mind wandering to thoughts of home. To the labyrinths of kelp and coral and the ocean currents running like avenues from pole to pole. To volcanoes glowing in the miles-deep dark, amid the lights of fish no man has ever seen.

Wrapped in our separate dreams, we lost track of time.

We forgot how hard it was in the water to hear any sound outside. The front door could have banged shut with a noise like a gun going off, and footsteps thundered on the wooden ramp, and we would have heard nothing.

Lulled by the silence, half-asleep, I caught a movement in the corner of my eye. I turned my head. There was a gap in the curtains covering the front of the tank.

Marcie was standing there, perfectly still, looking in.

I saw her red satin jacket, glowing like oil, and her wide, staring face. For one long, dreadful second our eyes met. As long as I live, I'll never forget her expression. It wasn't shock, or fear, or even surprise. It was greed.

Her whole face shone with it. The edges of the curtain were bunched in her fists, and her cheeks burned, redder than her jacket.

It was as if I'd seen her soul.

I jerked away, faster than light. When I looked back, Marcie was gone.

We scrambled out of the water, clumsy with panic, all too aware of the danger we'd caused by our carelessness. We knew we had to leave at once.

In the few minutes while our bodies turned and our skin grew dull again, we made our decisions. I would return to the ocean, but Aquabelle would remain on the land. There was no time to try to talk her out of that. Besides, I could tell it would have been useless.

I'd never seen her more

frightened — and yet more certain — of anything.

She wanted to be with Anthony, she told me. They
would go far away to a place where she
couldn't be found. She would live a
human life.

I accepted her choice, although
I didn't understand it. The ocean
had always been world enough for me.
And now that the time had come to go
back, I was longing to be gone.

We pulled on our clothes and ran hand in
hand down the ramp behind the tank, into the
dark props room below. Beyond lay the viewing
gallery, the front office — and freedom. We reached
the props room door and stopped short. Aquabelle
tried the handle.

It had been bolted from the outside. Marcie had
thought fast. She was ahead of us.

She was standing on the other side of the door.
I could hear her breathing. Aquabelle rattled the
handle. She raised her fists and beat on the wood
until I pulled her arm to make her stop. Then
Marcie began speaking.

What she'd seen in the tank, it didn't

surprise her, she said. She'd known we were special, and she would keep our secret. After all, it wouldn't suit her plans if people knew the truth. We would keep on performing, wearing our costumes and pretending to come up for air. But now that Marcie knew what we were capable of, we'd no longer be appearing at the Crystal Cove. She would sell the place, and create a new show for us, a show like no other.

Our new tank would be huge, Marcie told us, her voice rising with excitement. She could already see it in her mind's eye. High-tech lighting, a grotto glittering with semi-precious stones... maybe live animals too. A couple of tiger sharks, an electric eel. Perhaps jellyfish! Marcie's voice rose still higher. Could we imagine the effect of *that*? Hundreds of poisonous jellyfish drifting around us as we swam...

She sounded unhinged, I thought. As if she'd gone completely mad.

The show would be too big for Lastland Island, Marcie continued, her thoughts hurtling along. Too big for the town on the mainland, or even the nearest city. She would take it around the country, and then the world, performing in only the most glamorous cities. She'd always wanted to travel, to stay in four-star hotels and go to cocktail parties with celebrities. She'd fit right in because, after all, she'd be a celebrity herself...

Aquabelle found my hand in the dark.

'We'll never be part of it,' she said in her beautiful, clear voice. 'We'll never do what you say.'

'Oh, I think you will,' Marcie said, her voice thick with satisfaction. She explained that the camera she'd installed was motion-sensitive. It had turned on the minute we'd entered the tank, and recorded the whole of our late-night swim. She had the tape in her pocket. If we didn't do as she said, she would show it to the world.

Aquabelle and I looked at each other. We knew we had no choice.

Thirty

Marcie was never good at thinking things through. She locked us up in separate rooms, yet she gave no thought as to how to keep us there. The idea that we might get help from outside didn't seem to occur to her. For all her cunning, she was a very stupid woman.

She informed everyone that we'd been locked up because we owed her money. Aquabelle somehow managed to send a message to Anthony, and he immediately came and demanded that she be let out. There was nothing Marcie could do about it. Not long after, Aquabelle and Anthony returned to get me too. But this time, Marcie was prepared.

She told them they had come too late.

I'd been put in a small utility room at the back of the building. I didn't know Aquabelle had escaped until one of the other girls whispered the news to me through the keyhole.

The instant I knew she was safe, I was even more desperate to return home myself. The thought of waiting another day, another hour, even another minute, felt more than I could bear.

The utility room was one of the few places in the Crystal Cove with a window; a skylight, two or three metres above my head. It didn't look as if it had been opened for years, the frame stuck fast under layers of crusted paint. I thought perhaps it would come free with the help of the right tool.

I found a stepladder behind a pile of planks stacked untidily against the wall. I retrieved it, and set it up as silently as I could. It was too short, even when I was standing on the top. So I got down, fetched a tin of paint, placed it on the ladder, and then climbed up again with a screwdriver clenched between my teeth to open the window.

Standing on tiptoe, on top of the paint can, on top of the ladder, I managed to reach the window. I shoved hard at the frame and felt it give. I was about to shove it again, when one of the bolts holding the stepladder together snapped in half.

I might have guessed the thing was shoddy, like everything else in the Crystal Cove.

I don't remember falling. All I remember is not being able to get up again. Marcie's face filled my vision. Someone was saying they should call an ambulance.

'Certainly not!' Marcie said. 'She just needs rest...'

I lay in bed for three weeks, concussed and delirious. I dreamed of a lost ocean; of vast, abandoned caverns, and empty sea floors, and ghost towns of dead coral, whiter than bone. Far off, someone with a broken heart was crying, but when I woke up, it was my own face wet with tears.

Eventually the fever passed, and I recovered most of my strength, although my legs remained weak. I could pull myself up, and stand for only a few, teetering seconds. It was obvious

I couldn't perform, and Marcie, bitter with disappointment, quickly grew tired of looking after me.

One day, she came back with an old wheelchair she'd found in a skip.

'You'll have to start working for your keep,' she told me. 'There must be *some* use to having you around.'

I only found out much later about Aquabelle and Anthony coming back to get me. It had happened the day after the accident, when I was in bed, only half-conscious. They had a lawyer with them, and Marcie couldn't win by arguing. She didn't even try. Instead she took them to the utility room. She'd had time to set the ladder back up, and open the window, and even attach a scrap of my shirt to a nail, so it looked as if I'd torn it getting out.

I'd run away, Marcie said, and Aquabelle believed her. She knew how I longed for the sea.

The Crystal Cove was never the same again. Each year it grew shabbier, the shows less impressive, the visitors fewer. Damp hung in the air, and algae began its slow green march across the tank.

Bit by bit, Marcie was forced to sell her finery. The chandeliers, the silk shirts and the red satin jacket, until only the cowboy boots remained. Marcie wore them every day, no matter the weather. She kept the leather buffed, and the silver spurs polished. They were all she had left to remind her of the glory days of the Crystal Cove.

Except for me, of course.

Thirty-one

'Why didn't you leave?' Stella asked.

They had been talking for hours.

'Where would I have gone? I didn't have a single penny — or a single friend.'

'Why not back to the ocean?'

Pearl was silent, her face pinched.

'I just realised something,' Stella said. 'The older woman in your story — on holiday with my dad — that was Gramma! She told me Mum was a mermaid because she saw her in the show!'

Gramma was always right, Stella thought. One way or another.

'So all this time my mum thought you'd gone back,' she said. 'She never knew you were here.'

Pearl shook her head. 'And I couldn't contact her because I didn't know where she'd gone.'

'We lived about as far from the sea as it's possible to get,' Stella said.

'Perhaps she didn't want to be reminded,' Pearl suggested. 'She gave it up for love, but it must have been hard at times.'

Stella nodded, thinking of the painting in the spare room of their house.

'I wonder if she ever thought of me,' Pearl said.

'She did think of you!' Stella said, suddenly remembering. She reached for her jacket, lying at the end of the bed, and pulled out the sketch of the mermaid.

'She must have done it from memory.' Stella handed the drawing to Pearl. 'It *is* you, isn't it? I knew you reminded me of someone...'

Pearl didn't answer. She stared at the sketch.

'Now I see why she drew your hand flat like that,' Stella said. 'I thought maybe you were waving, but it's not a wave. It's your hand pressed against the front of the tank, isn't it?'

Pearl still couldn't speak. Tears rose in her turquoise eyes, and Stella thought of the jewels in

Gramma's lost bracelet, glinting through water, forever out of reach.

'Thank you for showing it to me,' Pearl said at last. She handed the picture back, although something of it had stayed with her. Her face had changed. She looked more like the girl in the drawing than ever before.

'You're kind, like your mother,' she said. 'Much kinder than I deserve.'

There was such friendship in her voice that Stella felt like crying.

'Why can't you help me?' she asked. 'Why can't you contact the police, or my dad... or anyone? Are you really that frightened of Marcie?'

'I daren't get the police involved. She has the video.'

'Anyone can fake a video.'

'But if they arrest me too, if they... investigate, what then? It's not just for me; I'm the least of it. Imagine what would happen if people knew we existed. They'd tear up the ocean looking for us; we'd never be safe. And they wouldn't stop until they'd destroyed us.'

Stella knew she was right. Pearl and her kind would be hunted down, every last one of them. They'd be made into trophies, imprisoned and experimented upon, dissected when they died. Stella thought of the specimen jars in the Natural History Museum, and she shuddered.

'Marcie could have made a lot of money if she'd used that video to expose me, although she never did,' Pearl said. 'Something happened to her that night, when she saw us in the tank. It messed up her mind. She was always a bad person, but I think the sight of us made her worse, drove her insane. She became obsessed with the idea that the Crystal Cove would be great again one day. Perhaps she hoped I'd get better, or that others of my people would come to find me. It wasn't much of a hope, but it was all she had.' Pearl paused. 'Until you showed up.'

Stella was speechless with sudden understanding.

'She wants me for the show, doesn't she?' It was so obvious; she didn't know why she hadn't guessed it already. 'She thinks... she thinks I'm—'

Her voice broke off. She couldn't bring herself to say the words aloud, although they were shouting in her head.

She thinks I'm the real fish.

Thirty-two

Stella's nanny Deb had a saying she'd been fond of repeating.

'Be careful what you wish for.'

At the time, Stella hadn't really known what it meant, unless Deb was talking about those fairy stories where people are given three wishes and end up wasting all of them. In that case, being careful what you wished for made a lot of sense.

Now the saying flashed into Stella's mind, and this time she understood its meaning perfectly.

She'd run away from home because she wished to know who — or what — she was. Yet now she'd give anything *not* to know. To be back home, alone and bored in her room, or fidgeting in the back of English class, or just staring out of the window of the bus as the land rolled by, flat and safe and unsurprising.

'It's not true,' she whispered. 'I can't change into anything. I'm *normal*.'

Pearl looked down at her hands.

Why hadn't help arrived? Stella thought in desperation. It had been ages since her phone call to Cam. Perhaps Cam hadn't picked up on the clue, after all. Stella tried to remember exactly what she'd said. She'd been forced to say she was with her mum's friends. She'd told Cam she was on Lastland Island; she'd made no mention of the Crystal Cove. Cam had seen the name when Stella showed her the drawing, although it was possible — even likely — that she hadn't remembered it. In that case, the police would have to comb the whole island to find her, and that would take time. But it also meant there was still hope.

'I know I'm normal,' she told Pearl with new courage. 'Nothing happens to me in the water. I used to swim a *lot* in our pool, and yesterday I went in the sea and I didn't feel different at all.'

Even as she spoke, Stella knew this wasn't quite true. Wading into the ocean, she'd felt odd, a bit light-headed. If the little boy with the bucket hadn't called out to her, she might have actually fallen. The waves had made her dizzy, she told herself. Or was it just hunger? It was hunger, after all, that had caused her to faint over tea with Pearl and Marcie.

'If I could... turn, I'd know it, wouldn't I?' she said.

For a moment, she thought Pearl wasn't going to answer.

'You asked me why I didn't return to the ocean. Marcie keeps a close eye on me, but I could have found a way to escape her. The truth is, I've always been too frightened to try. My body was so damaged by the accident that I don't know whether it can change in the water like it used to. And by the time I find out, it might be too late.'

'Why?' Stella said, dread rising.

'Because my body won't transform until... it has to,' Pearl said, stumbling over the words. 'Until something in me shuts down. That has to happen, you see, in order to trigger the turn...'

'I don't understand. *What* has to happen?'

Pearl hesitated for a second, her face contorted by anxiety.

'Humans call it drowning,' she said.

Pearl was still talking, although Stella couldn't hear her any longer. She was back in her dream, sinking towards endless darkness, the light no more than a pinprick above her head.

'Drowning?' she repeated.

Pearl's hands fluttered in agitation. 'There's no other way...'

Thirty-three

Somewhere beyond the walls of the Crystal Cove, morning must have arrived, although there was no evidence of it. Only the hand on Stella's watch, pointing to eight a.m. She had spent the night awake, tormented by her thoughts, unable to stop imagining what it would be like to drown, not in a nightmare, but in real life. And after she drowned, what then? Would she simply die, or would she turn instead? Her mind and body changing until she wasn't Stella Martin any more. Until she wasn't even human any more.

It was too much to take in, and after a while a dull despair settled over her. There was no use hoping the police were hunting for her. They would have found her by now if they were. The phone call to Cam had been pointless.

She should have used it to scream for help while she had the chance. She lay motionless on the bed, her eyes fixed on the far wall, not even lifting her head when the door opened and Marcie came in.

There was a dark red, trailing clump in one of Marcie's hands. It was a wig.

'Pearl is rustling up some breakfast,' Marcie told her, 'if you can call it that. The cupboard is bare, to say the least. Not a lot coming in from ticket sales. We get more cash out of the donation bucket.

Don't look at me like that,' she added, catching Stella's eye. 'People think they're giving to save the ocean, but if they really cared about it, why'd they mess it up in the first place?'

She took the wig and gave it a little shake. 'Stand up.'

Stella did as she was told, her legs moving numbly. Marcie tugged the wig over her head, jerking it into place. 'I've been hard at work, altering a couple of the old costumes for you,' she said, excitement filling her voice. 'I've still got a couple of finishing touches to make, and then we can have a fitting...' She stepped back. 'I think it suits you!'

In the cloudy mirror, Stella saw a familiar face gazing back at her. She had always longed to look like her mum. Now, with the red wig tumbling around her face, and her eyes wide with fear and surprise, she saw that she did. The resemblance was startling.

'I think we'll call you Little Aquabelle,' Marcie said.

'I'm not like her!' Stella cried, pulling at the wig. 'I'm *not!*'

'Well, we don't know that yet, do we?' Marcie said.

She thumped out of the room, leaving Stella staring after her. If Marcie had already nearly finished Stella's costume, she must be planning to try her out in the tank very soon.

There was no time left.

She had to escape. Staying was not an option. And if she couldn't rely on the police, or Pearl, or anyone else, she would have to do it alone.

She looked around the room. Surely there was something there she could use to get out. She'd been staring for hours at the two threadbare beds, the wardrobe, the light bulb dangling from its fraying cord. She could have described them with her eyes shut, down to the last detail. Yet maybe she'd missed something.

Perhaps she could make a weapon. The legs of the bed were too short for that. She could smash the mirror, and use one of the shards, except she had nothing to smash it with. Stella walked across the room and back again, looking for a chink in the wooden floorboards. Perhaps one was loose, although she wasn't exactly sure how that would help. But she found nothing.

She sat down on the bed again, feeling panic start to return.

I am going to get out of here, she told herself. *I have made up my mind.*

Slowly, she allowed her gaze to wander over the walls and ceiling of the room. She knew every crack, every ancient stain. On the wall by the door, there was a patch where the paint appeared different, the surface far rougher. Stella had noticed it before without giving it much thought. Now she wondered what lay underneath the paint to make it look that way. Could it be an area of crumbling plaster, a weakness?

It was only because she was staring at the wall so intently that she happened to notice a shadow, no more than a centimetre wide, running down the side of the door. It wasn't particularly remarkable in itself. What made it interesting was the fact that Stella was certain that it hadn't been there before.

It was exactly the kind of shadow a door might make, if it was no longer flush with the frame, but was very slightly open.

She got up, terrified she might be mistaken. But she wasn't.

Marcie had left the room with the wig in one hand, and her head full of plans. She had unlocked the door and gone through, pulling it shut behind her. Except she hadn't pulled it quite all the way.

Stella peered through the crack. She could see the latch. It was pressed in halfway, the weight of the door leaning against it. Even the slightest touch might be enough to send it home.

She stepped back and wiped her fingers on her shorts. She blew on them, and then, hardly daring to breathe, placed her fingertips against the wood, in the space where the door stuck out from the frame. She pulled gently, then pressed her fingers down harder and pulled again. There was a slight click as the latch came free. The door opened.

The corridor was empty, the light from a cracked wall sconce sending shadows across the thinly-carpeted floor, all the way to the door at the far end.

That was the route to the front of the building; through the kitchen and the viewing gallery, then up the ramp to the front office. Stella was about to step into the corridor, when she stopped. Pearl had told her that Marcie spent most of her time in the kitchen. If she was in there now, there was no possibility of getting past her.

But Stella might have a chance if Marcie thought she had already escaped.

It took all Stella's self-control to step back into the room, carefully leaving the door ajar. She tiptoed across the floor, suddenly grateful for the lack of furniture. The bareness of the room would make it seem empty. There was no place to hide.

Except for one. Stella opened the wardrobe and climbed inside. There was just enough room to close the door if she sat sideways, with her knees pulled up.

It was as dark as the back of the removal van had been. By the dim green light of her watch face, Stella retrieved the necklace from her pocket and fastened it around her neck. She had kept it hidden for fear Marcie would steal it. The chain was gold, and worth some money. But it didn't matter now, she was getting out. If she failed, losing the necklace would be the least of her worries.

It was a comfort to feel it in its usual place again.

The word of the sea. Stella had always wondered why her mum had called it that. *It's the best thing I have*, her mum had said.

Pearl might have known the reason, if Stella had asked her. It was too late now. Marcie would be coming back at any moment. The wire coat hanger rattled gently on the rail above Stella's head. She reached up and removed it, holding it tightly in the dark.

It wasn't much of a weapon, but it was all she had.

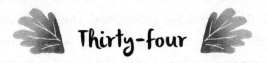

Thirty-four

Stella didn't have long to wait. Marcie returned barely five minutes later. Sound was muffled in the wardrobe, and Stella didn't hear her footsteps until they were right outside the room.

The steps advanced, and then stopped.

In the two or three seconds of silence that followed, Stella had time to wonder whether she had made a fatal mistake. Maybe she would have been better off making a dash for it, while she'd had the chance. She tightened her grip on the coat hanger.

Hiding in the wardrobe had been a bad idea. Anyone would think to check there.

But Marcie wasn't good at thinking, especially

when she was in a rage.

'Pearl!' she bellowed. 'PEARL!' She turned and rushed out of the room, her boots thundering.

Stella knew she had to stay hidden until the coast was clear. If she stayed *too* long, however, Marcie might change her mind and return to check the room. Stella decided to count to three minutes, yet she had only got to one and a half, when something else occurred to her. What if Marcie had slammed the door shut as she'd left? She remembered hearing a bang...

She clambered hurriedly out of the wardrobe and, to her relief, the door was wide open

Stella zipped her jacket all the way to the top and slipped into the corridor, as quietly as she could.

The door to the kitchen was ajar. Stella listened, her ear against the wood, and heard nothing. Quickly, before she had time to lose her nerve, she peered around the door, saw nobody, and darted inside.

She scurried across the pitted lino, heading for the door at the other side of the room. There was a pair of dressmaker's scissors on the kitchen table, and a heap of gaudy, sequined fabric. Little Aquabelle's costume, she thought with a shudder.

She had never wanted to run so much in her whole life. But the door leading to the viewing gallery was closed, and Stella didn't know who was on the other side.

She forced herself to be still, waiting for the slightest sound. She reached for the door handle and levered it down, opening the door, centimetre by centimetre.

The viewing gallery was deserted, but it worried her that she didn't know where Marcie was. If she suddenly appeared, she would see Stella straightaway. Yet Stella couldn't remain hovering by the kitchen door. She set off at a nervous trot, heading for the ramp at the far end of the gallery.

She had gone about six metres, when she heard a noise, a rapid thudding. It was coming from the front office. Stella froze in her tracks. She could hear the murmur of voices. One was Marcie's; she'd know that fake laugh anywhere.

Without pausing, Stella dashed back the way she'd come. There must be another way out. All buildings had back doors, didn't they? She passed the door to the kitchen, darted through another entrance, to the right of the curtain covering the big tank. She stood behind the door, not daring to close it in case somebody heard, her heart hammering.

She was in a room filled with clothes rails and untidy heaps of bric-a-brac. Plastic balls and buckets, a cardboard thunderbolt, piles of tangled fishing net, a sagging, inflatable shark and a dolphin in a state of similar collapse. The props room, she guessed. The door at the other end must lead up to the back of the tank. Pearl had described it when they were talking.

To the left, there was another door, a heavy-looking thing, partly open, with a metal bar in place of a handle. Stella couldn't spare it more than a glance. She could still hear voices, too low to make out any words, although getting louder by the second. Marcie was in the viewing gallery and, from the sound of it, she was heading directly her way.

Stella scanned the room, looking for a place to hide, decided against it, and ducked through the door with the metal handle instead. Her feet crunched. She was treading on sand. The air was thick with the smell of damp salt and bleach, and in the dim light filtering down from above, she saw the shapes of large rocks, piled to form a tower.

She was in the tank itself.

Apart from a couple of lingering puddles, the place was dry. The door must be designed to be watertight when the tank was full. But Stella didn't have any time to focus on details. Marcie had entered the props room, boots jangling.

'This is where we keep all our materials for the show,' she was saying. 'There's nobody here, as you can see...'

'Where does that door lead to?' someone said. 'Is it made of metal? Why is it so thick?'

Stella felt a surge of joy and utter dismay. She knew the owner of that voice. There was only one person who fired off questions like that, never able to wait for an answer before the next came shooting out.

'Stella!' Cam shrieked, stepping with a crunch of sand into the tank. 'There you are!'

Thirty-five

The tank door slammed shut, and she heard the scrape of the metal bar as Marcie locked it into place.

'Hey!' Cam said, whirling around. 'Why did she do that?'

'Are you on your own?' Stella cried. 'Isn't anyone with you?'

'I came by myself!' Cam told her, sounding triumphant. 'I worked it all out last night, and got the first ferry this morning, before anyone had got up. I remembered the name "Crystal Cove" from that drawing you showed me and—'

'Didn't you call the police, or tell anyone?' Stella interrupted.

'You said not to tell,' Cam said, her face starting to fall. 'You made me promise.'

Stella stared at her silently. She was wearing a long, navy trench coat that Stella guessed belonged to her mum. The collar was turned up, and there was a hat perched at a strange angle on one side of her head.

'Why are you wearing that hat?'

'It's not a hat, it's a beret. You know, like a French spy?'

'Oh, *Cam*,' Stella said.

'I've messed up, haven't I?'

'Kind of. I might've escaped if you hadn't shown up.'

'You mean, we're *kidnapped*?' Cam said, her face instantly brightening. 'Wow!'

'This isn't a game, Cam!'

'I knew that woman was shady, I knew it,' Cam said. 'She said you weren't here any more, but she could tell I wasn't convinced. That's when she offered to show me around so I could see for myself.

What a place,' she added. 'All those old costumes... so that's what you meant when you said your mum used to be a mermaid!'

Stella opened her mouth to tell Cam everything. About finding her way to the Crystal Cove, about seeing the video, and listening to Pearl's story, and the awful moment Stella had found out what Marcie was planning for her. She'd been longing for the chance to confide in Cam, partly to prove her wrong, but mostly for the sheer relief of being able to share the whole, incredible story with someone.

Yet she couldn't, no matter how much she wanted to. It wasn't just her secret, nor was it just Pearl's. It was far bigger than that. It was the ocean's secret. In that instant, Stella knew that she would never tell it. Even more, she would do anything in her power to protect it, whatever the cost.

'That's right,' Stella said, looking Cam steadily in the eye. 'With a tail and everything.'

'Cool,' Cam said. 'And I suppose you've been kidnapped for money... So how do we get out of here?'

In the light of day, the tank was a dingy sight. The plastic coral was drab and the sand lay in untidy heaps, mixed with old sequins and fragments of coloured glass, their sparkle no more than a memory. Cam ran her finger over the cloudy glass. Behind it, the curtain was drawn, blocking their sight.

Stella tried the door, although she knew it was pointless. She looked up. Ten metres over their heads, and a further metre above the top of the glass, she saw another door set into the wall of the upper storey, and a platform jutting over the edge of the tank.

It must be the platform she'd seen in the video, where the performers entered at the start of the show. Yet it was well above the water level when the tank was full. How did the mermaids with their cumbersome tails climb back out again?

'I think that platform — or part of it, anyway — can be raised and lowered,' she told Cam.

'What if we climbed the rocks?' Cam asked. 'Could we reach it from there?'

She scrambled quickly to the summit, then bent and hauled Stella the rest of the way.

There wasn't much room on the top of the tower. The girls had to stand close together, and every time they moved, the topmost rock wobbled. The platform was still a good couple of metres above them.

'Can you reach?' Stella asked.

'Maybe if I stood on your back...'

Stella bent her knees cautiously. The rock tilted beneath her shifting weight, and she straightened up again.

'It nearly fell,' she gasped. 'We have to keep still.'

Just then they heard a sound. A loud clank, immediately followed by a gurgling noise. They looked down. A dark, inky shadow was creeping over the floor of the tank. When it reached the glass, it rippled and spread sideways, sending long, gleaming ribbons racing to the farthest corners.

'Water!' Cam cried.

The sound grew louder. The water was gushing now, tumbling against the base of the tower, turning the rock shining black.

'Somebody must've turned it on by mistake!' Cam said. She raised her voice. 'Hey! Is anyone there? *Hey*!'

But Stella knew the water hadn't been turned on by mistake. Marcie knew exactly what she was doing.

The water was a metre deep already, the surface calmer than before, although rising steadily. A broom — used perhaps for sweeping sand — floated by, and lodged against the coral sculpture, creating a small eddy.

'I'm scared to swim,' Stella whispered. 'I haven't done it since...'

Cam removed the belt from her coat, and flung it wildly in the direction of the platform. The buckle pinged off the edge and the belt fell into the water, twisting like a snake.

'My mum's going to kill me,' she said.

She didn't get it, Stella thought. She was still acting as if this was some big adventure.

The water level reached the third rock of the tower, barely two metres below. A string of tiny bubbles rose above the coral from a hole in the plastic.

'Look at that!' Stella cried, pointing to the other side of the tank. It was a short steel ladder, with curved ends for latching on to a rail. It had been propped against the wall, but was now lying flat at the bottom of the tank.

'If only we'd seen that before,' Stella said. 'We could've hooked it on to the platform.'

'I can get it.'

'But you'd have to dive all the way down. And how would you bring it up?'

'Things are much lighter in the water,' Cam pointed out.

'Can you swim that far?'

'Easy!' Cam said, removing her beret with a flourish. She took off her coat and handed it to Stella. 'Guard this with your life,' she ordered. And suddenly, the things that Stella had found annoying about Cam — her big talk, her exaggeration, her drama — didn't seem annoying any longer, but just the opposite. Stella smiled, her spirits lifting. How could anything really bad happen with Cam around?

Cam had once swum the length of the school swimming pool underwater, and there was a good chance she would have been able to reach the ladder and haul it to the top of the tower too. She never got that chance. Just as she was about to dive, the platform overhead shook with an almighty clatter. The girls looked up.

Marcie was standing there, staring down at them. Pearl, in her wheelchair, behind her.

Thirty-six

'Finally!' Cam exclaimed. 'Didn't you hear me yelling?'

Marcie ignored her. She squatted on her heels, her spurs ringing against the metal struts of the platform. Her eyes narrowed as she assessed the rising water, then she looked at her watch.

'I'd say we've got about seven minutes,' she said, getting to her feet again. 'Don't you agree, Pearl?'

'Pearl!' Stella cried. 'Make her stop!'

Why wasn't she looking at Stella? Why was she just sitting there, her hooked stick in her lap, her face blank?

'Aren't they going to switch the water off?' Cam

asked. Stella could see dread beginning to dawn in her eyes.

'No, Cam, they're not.'

Cam clutched Stella's arm, making them both sway and almost lose their footing.

'But if they don't switch it off, we'll...'

Stella looked up at Marcie. 'Let Cam go. I'll do anything you want if you let her go.'

'I think you're going to do that anyway,' Marcie said, tilting her head as if she was talking to a very young child. 'Six minutes. Then we'll see what you're really made of, Stella Martin.'

'What's she talking about?' Cam demanded.

Stella shook her head. The water was creeping around their feet, turning the rock dark and slippery. She glanced beseechingly at Pearl, although she knew it was no use. How could she – in her wheelchair – fight Marcie?

'You won't get away with this!' Stella cried.

'I'll cross that bridge when I come to it,' Marcie said. 'I prefer to focus on the big picture.' She leaned over the water, her face avid. 'A new show for a new star! Think of the possibilities!'

Pearl was right, Stella thought. Marcie really *had*

been driven mad. Over the long, brooding years, the madness had only got worse.

Stella's feet were wet; the water was over her ankles, far colder than she expected. She looked at Cam.

'I'm sorry I laughed at you,' Cam said, her voice quiet. 'I knew I was being mean.'

'It's okay,' Stella said. 'Really, it is. Thank you for trying to rescue me.'

Cam nodded sadly. 'If I get out of here,' she said, 'I'll never go looking for drama or exaggerate anything ever again. Even if I live for a trillion years.

Even under *torture*,' she added.

Despite herself, Stella couldn't help smiling. 'I'll remember you said that.'

It wouldn't be long now. In a few seconds, the water would have risen past her knees. Stella took off her jacket and tied it at her waist. Her arms were shaking; she had to wrap them around herself to make them stop. Perhaps it wouldn't be as terrible as she imagined. Perhaps her body would turn. For all her longing to be normal, maybe she *was* of the sea. A hundred times wilder, and a hundred times more alien than any mermaid ever dreamed of.

She shivered.

But if she did turn, she'd be able to save Cam. There was that, at least.

Then she thought of her nightmare again. The helpless sinking. She clutched the stone around her neck, her breath coming fast and shallow. Why was Pearl staring at her like that, with such a fixed expression? Stella's legs suddenly felt too weak to support her weight, and she would have fallen if Cam hadn't flung a strong arm around her. A rushing sound filled her ears. Marcie said something, although Stella couldn't hear what it was.

'*Listen*,' Cam whispered.

Stella managed to lift her head.

'Be careful, Pearl,' Marcie was saying. 'Remember I have the tape.'

Pearl spoke, her voice too soft for them to make out the words.

'You try anything,' Marcie said, turning to face her, 'and you're going in there too.'

Stella couldn't see Pearl's face. Marcie was in the way.

'Lower the platform,' Pearl said, much louder than before. 'Do it at once.'

'Or what?' Marcie stepped sideways, her hands on her hips.

Stella could see Pearl clearly now. Her eyes looked dark, almost black, and there was something intent and fluid in the way she was sitting that made Stella suddenly hold her breath.

'What are you going to do?' Marcie jeered. 'Wave at me with your little stick?'

Marcie had grown so used to the crushed and broken figure in the wheelchair, she'd forgotten that in another life, Pearl had been quite different. In that life, Pearl had been stronger than the pull of the tides, and faster than an orca's leap, and her body still held the memory of that power.

She leaned down, and her arm shot out in a movement that was so swift and sudden, Marcie never glimpsed it coming. Nor did the girls, watching intently from below. All Stella saw was Pearl's stick as it struck Marcie's left boot, and the slight, upward flick of the hook catching the spur.

For a split-second, Marcie stood gaping, frozen in disbelief and confusion. Then, with a tightening of muscle, Pearl's arm jerked back again, and Marcie's foot shot out from under her. She hit the platform with a rattling crash, rolled, and fell into the tank.

Almost instantly, the platform began to lower towards the water.

'Quickly,' Pearl said.

Marcie was on the other side of the rock tower, her arms thrashing as she struggled to stay afloat. Stella glanced at her nervously, and then at the platform. It was at the level of the surface now. The water was still rising. Stella knew she was only seconds away from losing her footing.

'I can't get there,' she said, her breath juddering with panic. 'I'm frightened to swim...'

'You don't have to,' Cam said, pulling her off the tower and into the water.

'Quickly!' Pearl repeated.

Stella clutched at Cam, terrified of the sudden emptiness beneath her kicking feet. Then they were at the platform, and she was clinging to the railing. Cam pulled herself out and turned to help her. Pearl raised the platform until they were standing on the walkway by the upper door.

'Let's go!' Cam shouted.

'Not without Pearl.' Stella grabbed the handles of the wheelchair.

'We can't,' Cam said. 'She'll slow us down.'

'You don't understand, you don't know what Marcie will do… Pearl saved us, Cam!'

Stella jerked the chair around. Only when she was at the door did she dare to look back down. Marcie was no longer at the surface. Stella caught a glimpse of her through the water. She was bent double, her hands furiously tugging at one of her boots, trying to remove it as she sank.

Thirty-seven

Stella flew down the ramp behind the tank, pulled by the momentum of the speeding wheelchair. It was far harder to push it on the ground floor. Cam was halfway across the viewing gallery, while Stella was still navigating her way through the props room.

'Wait for me! Help me push!'

Cam ran back and took the other handle. Together, the girls manoeuvred the wheelchair through the gallery, into the front office and out into the street.

Stella stood for a second, dazed by relief to be in the open air. The sun was warm and a breeze brought the sound of music. How ordinary it all seemed, how unchanged. As if the last two days had never happened.

Even the Crystal Cove looked unremarkable, nothing more than a faded sign above a dusty window.

'We've got to find someone with a phone,' Cam was saying. 'I've got to call my parents, we've got to report this.'

Stella's grip tightened on the handles of the wheelchair. 'No,' she said. 'We can't, not yet.'

'That woman tried to kill us!'

'They'll arrest Pearl, they'll think she was part of it.'

'Well, wasn't she?'

'It wasn't her fault.'

Cam began walking fast up the empty street. Stella had to half-run to keep up with her, the wheelchair jerking and bouncing over the uneven surface.

'Leave me,' Pearl whispered.

'I can't,' Stella panted. 'You're not safe. You need to get far away from her.'

Cam had almost reached the crossroads with the main street.

'We'll get the ferry,' Stella begged her. 'The minute we get to the mainland, I'll call my dad, I promise.'

Once, a long time ago, her dad had swung her from the edge of the swimming pool, his arms strong and sure. The memory came back to Stella so suddenly and so vividly, that her eyes swam with tears.

'My dad will know what to do. He'll sort everything out.'

Cam hesitated. 'Okay,' she said at last. 'If you promise... I have a bad feeling about this,' she added, as they turned on to the main street. Stella was walking too fast to answer her.

'A bad, bad feeling,' Cam repeated.

Stella tried to remember exactly where the pier was, and guessed they weren't far away. She quickened her pace, although the nearer they got to the town centre, the more pedestrians there were, and she had to keep slowing down. She couldn't help noticing that many of them looked at her, staring as she hurried along, the wheelchair bumping. They stared at Cam as well, but Stella was too anxious to pay much attention.

'Do you remember when the ferry leaves?'

She couldn't hear Cam's reply. There was too much noise around them. Lastland Island was getting ready for the evening. Neon signs buzzed and flicked into life, fudge poured like lava into waiting trays, street musicians tuned up their instruments and a thousand glow sticks sprouted from waiting stalls.

Stella noticed a giant red lobster on a sign. She remembered seeing it the day she arrived.

'The pier's just down there!'

They struggled through the crowds, and turned at last on to the boardwalk leading out to the marina. The sun was low over the sea, the water a pale, electric blue, and there lay the ferry, docked like a miracle at the very end of the pier.

Stella began to run, although as she grew closer to the ferry, she saw there was no need to hurry. There was a long queue waiting to embark.

'Wheelchair coming through!' Cam called, and the queue parted to let them pass. In a moment they would be over the metal gangplank, on their way to home and safety...

'Tickets, please!'

Stella felt her stomach tighten. She had completely forgotten about tickets. You were meant to buy them at a booth on the pier. But even if they had time to turn around and make their way back, it wouldn't be any use. She had no money left. She had used it up getting into the show at the Crystal Cove. And by the stricken look on Cam's face, it was obvious that Cam didn't have any money either.

'Tickets,' the man repeated, already looking past them.

'We... we don't have them,' Stella said helplessly.

The man made a gesture of impatience. 'You can't board without tickets.'

'We *do* have them,' Cam said in desperation. 'We just can't show them to you.'

'Why not?'

'Because...' Cam's glance fell on Pearl. 'Because my mum is sitting on them!' she said wildly.

'Sitting on them?'

'She wanted to keep them safe. She always sits on things she wants to keep safe,' Cam said, starting to enjoy herself. 'Letters, passports, car keys, you name it.'

She leaned towards the man, her voice dropping to a whisper. 'Last week we found three silver forks and my dad's whole coin collection under there. Can you believe it?'

The man cleared his throat and eyed Pearl nervously. 'Ma'am? I really do have to see those tickets...' Pearl stared back without blinking. 'Ma'am, if you could just...'

Pearl folded her arms and narrowed her eyes.

'I think you're upsetting her,' Cam said. 'She's getting upset, isn't she, Stella?'

Stella nodded.

'Bad things happen when she gets upset,' Cam said.

'Well, I don't know,' he said, 'but you can't hold everyone up like this.' And he hurriedly waved them through.

'*My dad's whole coin collection?*' Stella hissed as they made their way on board. 'You always go too far.'

'It worked, didn't it?'

They wheeled Pearl into the lounge and found an empty bench, tucked out of sight of the other passengers. It wasn't until Stella had parked the wheelchair and sat down that she realised why she and Cam had been getting such odd looks, ever since leaving the Crystal Cove.

'We're still completely wet through,' she said. 'I never even noticed!'

Thirty-eight

The ferry was busy and it was a good fifteen or twenty minutes before everyone had boarded and the engines started. Stella let out a long breath, reassured by the feeling of water moving beneath her. The ferry turned slowly in the harbour, then picked up speed, heading for the open sea.

'I'm going to lie down for a minute,' Cam mumbled, stretching her long legs out on the bench, and in thirty seconds she was fast asleep. Stella gazed through the window as the land grew further away. Her shoulders relaxed, and she untied her jacket from around her waist.

'Do you want a drink of water?' she asked Pearl.

Pearl was staring at the horizon. Stella wondered how she could gaze so steadily at the glittering, sunlit sea without squinting.

'No,' Pearl said, not turning her head. 'Just a paper napkin.'

'A napkin?' Stella hesitated, wondering if Pearl was unwell. But she didn't look ill. There was colour in her cheeks, a faintest wash of pink beneath her silvery skin. Stella made her way to the bar on the other side of the lounge. She had to wait for several minutes, but when she returned, Pearl hadn't moved.

'I brought you a few,' Stella said, laying them on the table next to her.

'One will be enough.'

Cam was lying on the bench, her right arm flung above her head, the other trailing on the floor. Even asleep, Cam couldn't help being dramatic, Stella thought.

'I'm going out on deck,' she told Pearl.

She leaned over the railing, her damp hair drying in the wind, the surface of the water flying by below. The ocean would never be the same again. Now, she knew that somewhere, deep below those waves, there were nameless beings, beyond the need for words or language. They had always been there, too swift to be caught, too cunning to be trapped, each cell in their bodies able to think, and feel, and understand. Her own mum had been one of them. For a moment, Stella wondered again what it might be like if she was one herself.

Alive, she thought. *More alive than I can dream of.*

Then she pushed the thought aside. She didn't need to know. It wouldn't matter if she never found out. Even so, she couldn't drag her eyes from the water. She leaned further over the rail, peering through the glittering swell. Right at that moment, far beneath, there might be one who watched, who saw the ferry passing, the brief flicker of Stella's shadow running over the surface of the waves.

'Can you hear it?' Stella straightened up. Pearl was beside her. The colour was deeper in her cheeks, and the wind had whipped her hair into a cloud.

'Hear what?'

'Listen.'

Stella tilted her head, catching the noise of seagulls, the steady hum of the boat's engines, the slap and hiss of passing waves.

'I hear the ferry...'

'Can't you hear the singing? Coming from all around?'

Stella looked at her uncertainly.

'It's the water,' Pearl said.

The sun was lower now. Lastland Island had vanished, and there was nothing as far as the eye could see to break the long blue line of the horizon. Far in the distance, something moved; a wisp of cloud or spray just above the surface. Stella blinked and it was gone.

'I have to go,' Pearl said.

'Where?' Stella asked, although she had guessed already.

'I should have done it years ago. Being on land drained my courage. But it will only take a moment, and anyone can be brave for a moment, can't they?'

'You could die!'

'Maybe.'

'But you're safe now!' Stella protested. She looked around. The deck was full of passengers, and in the last few moments more had arrived, crowding the railings and the space around the wheelchair.

'You're safe,' Stella repeated, lowering her voice. 'Marcie can't hurt you any more, and my dad will work out what to do. He knows you, remember? He'll help you. You were my mum's best friend.'

'I don't want to be safe,' Pearl said. 'I want to be free.'

Stella stared at her in silence for a moment.

'I can't do it here,' Pearl said, speaking rapidly. 'I can pull myself out of the chair by holding on to the boat rail, then slide under the lowest bar. But it'll take me a few minutes. Someone will see and pull me back before I even get halfway.'

Stella remembered her journey to the island. The ferry had been busy that day too. Though she'd been on the lower deck, where there weren't any seats and only a few passengers.

'I know where it's quieter,' she said. She hesitated. Then she thought of her mum's drawing. The mermaid with her hand against the glass, unable to turn away, though her eyes were filled with longing to be gone.

'There's hardly anyone on the lower deck,' she told Pearl, her voice quiet. 'I can take you there, if you like.'

Pearl's face flooded with gratitude and relief. A seagull wheeled low over the deck. Suddenly her eyes widened and all the colour left her cheeks.

'What is it?'

'She's here,' Pearl said. 'She's followed us.'

Thirty-nine

Stella turned, felt a hand grip her shoulder, saw Marcie's face, frighteningly close.

'You ruined my boots!'

It ought to have sounded ridiculous. But there was nothing funny about the rage in Marcie's voice, or the mad look in her eyes. Her cheeks had darkened to purple, and her hair was plastered to her skull in flat, grey strips. She had flung an old army jacket over her wet clothes, together with a grubby-looking bag.

'I knew you would be on the ferry, I knew it!'

'Let go of me,' Stella said. 'Let go or I'll scream.'

'Scream all you like,' Marcie said, although she removed her hand.

'You can't do anything to us,' Stella said, yet there was a tremble in her voice. Even here, in the relative safety of the ferry, with people around, Marcie still had the power to terrify her. But Marcie was only one person, Stella told herself. There was no reason to be frightened of her now. 'You can't do anything,' she repeated, more fiercely.

'I don't want to do anything,' Marcie said, her mouth twisting as she tried to control her fury.

'So why are you following us? What do you want?'

'I want her,' Marcie said, jerking her head in the direction of Pearl. 'I'm taking her back to the Crystal Cove, where she belongs.'

Stella clenched her fists. 'Pearl won't go with you, she's not your possession!'

'Maybe not, but she's my insurance.'

'What do you mean?'

'So long as she's with me, I'm betting you won't be doing any tattletaling about our little… escapade,' Marcie said. 'Not when you consider what a story I'd have to tell if you called the authorities.' She patted her bag with a meaty hand. 'I have a copy of the tape right here, as a matter of fact. Hard to argue with evidence like that.'

'You can't take her. I'll stop you!'

'It's no good. I have to go with her, don't you see?' Pearl suddenly looked as washed out as she had the first time Stella had seen her, in the sickly light of the Crystal Cove.

'I could tell everyone right this minute, that you tried to kill us,' Stella told Marcie. 'All I have to do is shout.' She looked around the deck. Several of the other passengers were already giving Marcie curious looks. 'They'd call the police. You wouldn't be allowed to take Pearl back. You wouldn't even be allowed off the boat.'

Marcie shrugged. 'You could do that,' she said. 'You're right, I'd be arrested. But I'd make sure Pearl was too, and I'd still have the tape. I think the police would be very interested to find out what kind of a monster she really is.'

A look of triumph swept Marcie's mottled face.

'You needn't worry. I'll take very good care of her,' she said. 'Although from now on, she'll have to do the chores without that little stick of hers.'

The thought of Pearl going back to the drudgery and torment of the Crystal Cove was more than Stella could bear. Yet the alternative was even worse.

If Marcie was arrested, Pearl would be exposed, and the secret of the ocean revealed to the world.

'The clock is ticking,' Marcie said. 'Any minute now, your friend will wake up, and you won't have the choice any longer.'

She was right. Cam would raise the alarm the instant she saw Marcie.

'What's it to be?' Marcie insisted, her voice charged with fear and impatience. 'Decide!'

Stella couldn't. She stood rigid, deaf to the sound of gulls and waves, the chatter of passengers, the throb of the ferry's engines.

If only there was another option — any other option.

She glanced at Pearl. How close she'd come to escape! If Marcie had appeared only a few minutes later, there would have been nothing she could've done. It was true she had the tape, but without Pearl, the tape was worthless.

What was it Pearl had said? *I don't want to be safe, I want to be free.*

Stella cast a quick look around. The deck was even more crowded than before. A dozen people would spot Pearl the moment she tried to move. Unless…

Stella took a deep, frightened breath. Unless.

Unless everyone on deck – everyone on the entire ferry – happened to be looking in the opposite direction when she did it.

Hadn't Stella told herself she would do anything in her power to protect the ocean's secret? Whatever the cost?

She bent down and touched Pearl's shoulder.

'Be free,' she whispered. Then she slid out of her trainers, and before Marcie had time to react, raced across the deck, swerving around benches and passengers until she reached the other side. Without a second's hesitation, she grasped the rail with both hands, put one foot on the lower bar and swung herself up.

The danger was very great. But the secret was worth it.

At least, she thought, *I'll find out who I really am.*

In the split-second before she jumped, poised between the sunset-streaked sky and the black water below, a realisation shot through Stella's mind with the force and clarity of utter truth. It was that her entire life, one way or another, she had been running away from this moment. And yet, without knowing, she had been running straight towards it all along.

She pushed off the rail as hard as she could, and leaped with outstretched arms into the sea.

forty

Stella had taken a huge breath, but she instantly lost it in the shocking coldness of the water. The force of her leap sent her body plunging, then she rose, her head breaking the surface, her eyes half-blinded by the splash and spray. She glimpsed the vast side of the ferry, the thrash of its wake, the shapes of figures along the rail, heard the yelling of a distant voice.

'Man overboard!'

She gasped, caught half a breath, her arms beating. The ferry sounded its horn with a long, ear-splitting blare, although Stella barely heard it. She was too busy battling to stay afloat. She struck out in the direction of the ferry, swimming with all her might, although within a few seconds it was clear she was making no headway. From the deck, the swell had looked small, almost gentle. Up close, it rose and fell in tall peaks, moving with irresistible force. Terror engulfed her. She kicked out, limbs flailing. Yet the water was too big to fight. It shoved against her with a smothering weight, reducing her movements to a flutter, silencing the cry in her throat.

A splash appeared next to the ferry, then two more in rapid succession. But Stella could no longer lift her head to look. Her legs stopped moving. She pushed against the water with the palms of her hands, as if trying to lever herself up, gave one last, desperate glance towards the sky, then slipped below the surface without a sound.

She struggled for a bit, her arms reaching weakly. But the pull of the darkness below was too strong, and after a few seconds she grew still. She drifted further beneath the surface, her back up and her legs stretched out in front of her, as though carried on an invisible chair, and now when she tried to move, she found she couldn't. Her body was shutting down; her heart slowing, even her eyelids refused to blink.

I am drowning, she thought, as she sank through the dimming water. *Will it happen now? Will I turn?*

She looked at her legs and found the answer. White skin, bruise on one knee, mole above the ankle of the left foot. Her legs, the same as they always were. Unturned, unchanged.

Human. Normal. Pure relief welled up in her, and hand in hand with the relief, a quiet yet terrible sadness.

I am going to die.

It seemed as though she was falling down the side of a great black, glistening wall, smooth in places, in others marked with strange white lines, like runes scratched in stone a thousand years ago. There was a window in the wall; something glittered in its shining glass. A green light, as brilliant as a star. Stella stared, struggling to make sense of it despite her failing vision.

It wasn't a window at all.

It was an eye.

Then the wall moved, and the world turned upside down.

forty-one

To the crew and passengers on board the ferry, it was a miracle. So much so, that for the rest of their lives, whenever they heard the word, they would immediately think of the events of that day. And no matter how long they lived, it would always be the miracle to which every other miracle was compared and found wanting.

A moment after Stella jumped, and the ferry halted and sounded its warning, three passengers, including a former Olympic swimmer, dived into the sea after her. As the ferry captain waited, her hands shaking slightly, to turn the vessel, and another crewmember scrambled to the bow with a life jacket, the three swam as fast as they could in Stella's direction. Along the deck rail, people clustered, pointing and shouting directions.

'It was a child!' someone said, and as the word spread, groans and cries could be heard. Passengers clutched at each other, muttering prayers under their breath, or jostled for a better view.

Then the speck that was Stella's head disappeared from sight. The swimmers paused, before redoubling their speed, although it was clear they no longer knew what to do next.

A silence fell on the deck of the ferry. One of the swimmers dived suddenly, only to rise seconds later, his hands empty. The passengers along the boat rail leaned forwards, their gaze fixed in desperate concentration on the water, searching for the smallest movement, the slightest sign of hope.

The first indication that something strange was about to happen came from the three people in the water. Although they were a short distance away from each other, they all stopped swimming at precisely the same moment and began to tread water, looking about them with an air of uncertainty. To the watchers on deck, it seemed as if each of the three had sensed something, or felt a kind of disturbance, although what it was, nobody knew. The sea looked exactly the same as it had done the moment before.

Then, one by one, each passenger noticed a difference in the area of water lying on the ferry's starboard side. At first it was no more than a change of texture, a calming of the swell in that particular spot. Half a second later, and there could be no doubt; a vast patch of the sea had grown utterly still, as flat and as glassy as if it had been covered with a layer of oil.

The three swimmers had stopped treading water and were now swimming away from the boat with frantic, splashing speed. But nobody on deck gave them a glance. Something shadowy was rising to the surface, something so vast that no one could sense its shape, or see where it began or where it ended.

'Whale!' a man suddenly bellowed.

It broke the surface with a mighty exhalation, a single breath so massive and yet so steady, it was almost a sigh, and a spout of air and condensed water vapour shot into the sky. The sea gleamed solid.

'Whale!'

It was by far the largest ever seen in those — or

any — waters, with a body that stretched like a shining highway, three times longer than the ferry and twice as wide. It had been drawn into the area, off its normal, far-off path, over two days before, and had been cruising offshore ever since, as though waiting for something.

A great cry burst from the watchers on the deck. There, looking tiny on the creature's enormous back, they saw a girl. She was lying face down, her cheek pressed against the whale's wet skin, her arms spread out as if in an embrace.

Cam leaned so far over the crowded boat rail that she almost tumbled overboard herself.

'Stella!' she screamed.

forty-two

Stella was still unconscious when the whale slipped noiselessly below, and human hands lifted her to safety. When she woke, she was lying on the deck of the ferry in an agony of coughing, a sharp pain in her chest. Faces loomed over her. She looked desperately for Cam, glimpsed her briefly, tried to talk.

'Oxygen,' somebody said, fitting a mask to her face.

An ambulance was waiting on the mainland. Stella twisted in protest as she was lifted on to a stretcher and hurriedly wheeled off the ferry. She needed Cam; she *had* to speak to her. But everyone around her was moving too fast.

In the hospital, doctors lifted her eyelids, and felt her pulse, and hooked her to machines to measure the zigzagging patterns of her brain and heart. Then they gave her something that sent her to sleep.

She woke next morning, her head clear. She sat up, her fingers automatically moving to her throat, her heart thumping in panic. A nurse entered, carrying breakfast on a tray.

'My necklace! Where is it?'

'It was taken off last night,' a nurse said. 'Look, it's right here, on the table next to you.'

Stella fastened it hastily around her neck.

'You're the girl who was rescued by a whale!' the nurse said, setting down the tray. 'It was all over the news last night. What happened? What was it like?'

'I don't remember.'

'What, nothing?'

Stella shook her head firmly. 'Nothing.'

A little later, the door flew open and Cam rushed in.

'They wouldn't let me see you until now! Are you okay? What's that tube thing stuck in your arm?'

'Cam—'

'My parents are outside. They're acting weirdly nice. I should run away from home more often.'

'Cam—'

'You'll never guess who was on the ferry with us,' Cam chattered, plumping down on the bed. 'Can you move your legs a bit? That's better... That mad woman who tried to kill us! She was keeping out of sight, but I spotted her, just before the ferry docked. I got the captain to call the police straightaway.'

Cam paused for an instant to relish the importance of her role in the event.

'I had to go to the police station to give a statement. They grilled me for hours.'

'But what happened to *Pearl*?' Stella burst out, finally managing to get a word in edgeways.

Cam looked down. 'I don't want to get you upset. They told me not to get you upset.'

'You have to tell me, Cam. Did you see her?'

Cam shook her head. 'Nobody did. She wasn't on the ferry when we landed. I'm sorry, Stella... They found her wheelchair. They think she must've fallen overboard too, somehow.'

Stella leaned back against the pillow.

'So she's gone...'

'Don't say that!' Cam clutched the bed covers with an anxious hand. 'They couldn't go back to look because it was already nearly dark, but they'll look today. Maybe they'll find her, maybe she didn't drown.'

Stella imagined Pearl clinging to the boat rail, finding her moment of courage. Had she heard the water singing as she fell? And had she turned, nameless and darkly strange below the shadow of the ferry, and become herself again at last?

'Yes, maybe,' Stella said, her eyes shining. 'Maybe.'

'I still don't understand how you ended up in the sea,' Cam said. 'What happened? Were you frightened when you saw the whale?'

Stella shook her head. 'I don't remember anything,' she said, although it wasn't true.

She remembered all of it. She lay quietly after Cam had gone, her mind reliving her jump off the ferry, her struggle, her breathless drift down. Then she thought of her mum and the gift she had inherited from her.

No mermaid tail, despite Marcie's twisted hopes and dreams. Instead, a necklace with a curious stone.

Her mum had called it the word of the sea.

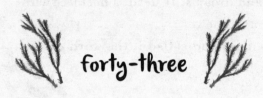

forty-three

Stella's dad arrived that afternoon. She was dressed and waiting for him in the hospital lobby. He hugged her and kissed the top of her head.

Stella tried to say how sorry she was, but she couldn't speak. He was holding her too tightly.

'Gramma will be pleased to see you,' he said, letting go at last. 'She was asking for you just this morning.'

'I thought she didn't know who I was,' Stella said. 'I thought she'd forgotten me.'

Her dad looked at her thoughtfully. 'I don't think your gramma has forgotten anything,' he said. 'I believe her memories are in there somewhere. She has trouble finding them when she needs to, that's all.'

Stella looked down at the ground, feeling the prickle of tears.

'She loves you,' her dad said, his voice gentle. 'Even if she sometimes isn't quite sure who you are.'

'Or *when* you are,' he added. 'Do you know what she said to me yesterday? She said I had to tidy my room, and if everything wasn't put away neatly, I wouldn't get any pocket money!'

Stella laughed and wiped her eyes with the back of her hand at the same time.

'I shouldn't have run away...'

'It was my fault,' he said, his own eyes glistening. 'I loved your mum so much. I was so busy missing her, I didn't see how much you were missing her too.'

Stella wanted to tell him that her mum had loved him as well, far more than he knew. Her mum had given up everything else in the world she loved — a whole other existence — just to be with him. But she couldn't. She couldn't tell anyone the truth, not even him, though it hurt her not to.

'I've been in a kind of dream,' her dad said. 'It took this — it took *you* to wake me up.'

He doesn't always know the right thing to say, you know, Gramma had once told her. *But he has a very good heart.*

Gramma never knew what she was talking about, Stella thought. Yet somehow, she was always, always right.

In the lobby of the hospital, people came and went, talking in quiet voices. The revolving door spun, a man sitting in a chair turned the page of his magazine, somebody coughed. Stella felt a surge of extraordinary happiness. Nothing was different, and yet everything in the world had changed.

'Can we go home now?' she asked.

forty-four

Stella stood up to her waist in the swimming pool, her back to the deep end, the sun hot on her shoulders. She had been in the pool every day since getting home, nearly two weeks before.

The first thing she had done when she arrived back, almost before the front door had closed behind her, was run upstairs and knock on Gramma's door.

It opened at once, as if Gramma already knew she was there.

'Where were you?' Gramma said. 'Did you miss the bus?'

She had just washed and dried her hair. It looked like a fluffy halo, lit up from the rays of the early morning sun.

'Oh, Gramma!' Stella cried, hugging her. 'I missed you so much!'

'I'm just about to have some breakfast,' Gramma said. 'Why don't you join me?'

'What has Mrs Chapman made today?'

Gramma lowered her voice. 'Poor Mrs Chapman hasn't been herself these last few days, but this morning she seemed very excited about something or other, said she was going to make her special blueberry pancakes...'

'Such a lot of strange things have happened to me, Gramma.'

'How very unsettling,' Gramma murmured. 'Do you want to tell me about it?'

'I can't,' Stella said. 'I wish I could, I've been wanting to tell someone so badly.'

'Well,' Gramma said, picking up her knitting, 'I expect I'd forget it the minute you told me, or muddle it up somehow.' She leaned forward conspiratorially. 'Between you and me, I'm getting a bit absent-minded, you know. It's rather difficult, although it does have some advantages. It means I'm very good at keeping secrets.'

So, with a feeling of great relief, Stella sat down on

the sofa and told her everything. It took a long time, and Gramma listened all the way through. Sometimes she said, 'My goodness!' or, 'How dreadful!' or, 'To think!' and sometimes she said nothing, but simply squeezed Stella's hand, her eyes full of concern.

When Stella was finally finished, Gramma sat silently for a while, a far-off look on her face.

'What are you thinking about?'

'I'm thinking how very proud of you your mum would be,' Gramma said. She paused. 'How silly! I'm crying!'

'I love you, Gramma,' Stella told her.

Gramma wiped her eyes, her face suddenly brightening. 'Did I tell you there are blueberry pancakes for breakfast? Mrs Chapman is cooking up a *storm*.'

'I was thinking of starting swimming again,' Stella said. 'Do you think it's a good idea?'

'I don't see why not,' Gramma said. 'It's terribly good exercise, you know.'

Stella's dad had the tarp removed that afternoon, and by the end of the next day, the pool had been cleaned and filled with water.

Stella kept to the shallow end to begin with. She

waded slowly across the pool, and back again, trailing her hands in the water. Then she swam a width and rested, panting against the side.

On the second day, she managed a whole length.

On the third, she held her nose, breathed in as deeply as she could, and sank below the water until her knees were resting on the floor.

Now she had decided to see whether she had the nerve to lie on her back and float. She would do it in the deep end, she thought, out of her depth, where she would have to trust the water to keep her buoyant.

She took a cautious step backwards. There was a place where the floor of the pool shelved steeply, and she was waiting to feel it beneath her feet before attempting to float.

She was about to take another, even more hesitant step, when her dad appeared, carrying a package in one hand and his phone in the other. He squatted by the edge of the pool, looking down at her.

'How would you like to move house?' he said.

'You mean, like nearer to my school?'

'No,' he said. 'Further away from your school. A lot further, as a matter of fact.'

Stella didn't understand. She stood still in the middle of the pool, staring at him.

'I'm going to be doing a different job,' he said. 'No more travelling for work. And we can live anywhere we like.'

His face was just as serious as it always was, although Stella could see the beginnings of a smile. 'I ought to have asked you first,' he continued, 'but I'm pretty sure I already know where you'd like to live, so I went ahead and put in an offer on a house.'

'Where?' Stella said, hope shrinking her voice to a whisper.

'Right on the beach,' her dad said. He was smiling properly now. 'Just down the hill from your friend Cam. You'll be able to go to school together.'

'Really?'

He nodded. 'Really.'

'*Really*?' Stella repeated. Then, 'But what about Gramma? And Mrs Chapman?'

'There's plenty of room for them too,' her dad said. He stood up, placing the package he was carrying on the side of the pool. 'I almost forgot. This came for you in the post this morning. It looks like it's from Cam's mother.'

He walked back up the lawn to the house. Stella splashed her way to the pool ladder as fast as she could.

The package was wrapped in brown paper, with Cam's return address on the back. Stella could feel something soft inside. She opened it and pulled out an item of clothing.

It was her jacket. The one she'd been wearing when she ran away. Cam must have found it on the ferry, and then forgotten to give it back to her in all the excitement.

Stella held it up. Despite its soaking in the tank at the Crystal Cove, the jacket looked perfectly fine. The only thing different was a bulge in one of the pockets. Stella undid the button, her fingers reaching inside.

She knew what it was the instant she touched it.

A paper napkin, folded small. A letter.

forty-five

Dear Stella,

By the time you read this, I will be
gone.

    I need to explain something, and this is the
easiest way.

    I told you once that your mother was born far
more human than the rest of us. The most human
thing about her was her overwhelming desire to discover
new things. It put her in danger, even in the ocean.
Because of this, she was given a treasure to keep her safe.
As long as she had it, she would always be protected in
the sea.

I didn't know you had that treasure until today, when you and your friend were in the tank. I wanted to save you from Marcie, but when I saw the stone around your neck, I knew I must, whether I wanted to or not. The word of the sea is unbreakable. As long as it is in your possession, you can come to no harm in the ocean. A million souls, from the great to the small, will always be there to help and protect you.

I only wish it could have protected your mother on land, as it did in the sea. Yet I know she never regretted her choice. She understood — as I should have done years ago — that the only life worth living is the one you live as yourself.

Pearl

Stella closed her eyes, no longer aware of the sun burning the back of her neck, the drip of her wet swimming costume. She was thinking about the aquarium, how the school of fish had suddenly changed direction, and how the turtle had seemed to follow her. And later, on the ferry, how the dolphins had found her shadow and kept pace with it for as long as they could.

Then she remembered the whale, and the way it had gazed at her, a green star burning in its watchful eye.

She hadn't known how long she had hung there, suspended in the water. Time had grown so slow that she could track the creeping path of each thought as it formed.

It wasn't a star. It was the reflection of something.

With the very last of her strength, she had managed to tilt her head and look down. The stone at her neck was glowing so brightly that it lit up the water. She was floating in a green fire.

Keep it safe, her mum had said. At least, that's what Stella had thought she said. But Stella had remembered it wrong. Her mum had been trying to tell her something quite different.

It's the best thing I have, she had said. *Keep you safe*.

The whale shifted a fraction, sending Stella tumbling head over heels. Then her body was caught and held by a massive force, solid as a continent. A thunder filled her ears, a rushing, and in the split-second before her senses faded, the roar of a mighty breath, as if the world itself had come up for air.

The sea had kept its word, its unbreakable promise.

Stella folded the napkin carefully, and returned it to the pocket of her jacket. She padded back to the pool and slipped in, moving without hesitation to the place where the floor shelved and grew deep.

Then she lifted her face to the sky and floated.

Acknowledgements

Writers write books, but editors make them worth reading. I owe a huge debt of gratitude to Fiona Kennedy for her brilliance and her unending patience.

Also to Rebecca Carter, agent extraordinaire, and all the people who put up with me on a daily basis, my sisters, my long-suffering sons, and my miraculously sane and supportive husband.

Tania Unsworth
2018

Readers' notes

Writing Style

Title

Discuss: What does the title tell you about the kind of book this will be? Does the title imply doubt in the girl's belief? Look at the artwork on the cover. Do you like it? Why?

Which genre is the book? Have you heard of the term 'magical realism'? Does this book fit into that genre?

Opening

'The first time Stella Martin ran away, it was in her sleep. The second was by accident. But the third time she did it on purpose, to find out whether she was human or not' (page 1).

Discuss: What do you think of the opening of the book? What does the author mean by 'The second was by accident'? Can you run away by accident? Think about the phrase 'to find out whether she was human or not?' What does it mean to be human?

Read the first chapter.

Discuss: Why does Tania Unsworth start the story with Stella's dream of drowning?

Water words

Tania Unsworth uses lots of water words within the story. Look again at the first chapter and see how she uses words linked to water to describe things: the marble as looking like liquid, the grass wet from the sprinklers, the swimming pool, and Stella's father sunk in his trance of sorrow.

Discuss: Why does she do this? Does it continue throughout the novel?

Activity: Choose one chapter and see how many times words connected with water are used. When are they used to describe water, and when are they used as metaphor? Look at the following sentences to help you:

'Stella's dad... sunk in his trance of sorrow' (page 2).

'nothing but the occasional water tower to cast a shadow' (page 6).

'Stella has a tendency to drift' (page 15).

'Stella was caught by a wave of grief and longing' (page 42).

Sounds

All writers use the senses to develop their descriptions and enhance the readers' empathy with the characters. This is called dynamic description. But in *The Girl Who Thought Her Mother Was a Mermaid*, there is a particular emphasis on sounds, or lack of sound.

Think about episodes in the book in which noise helps Stella, or in which she has to stay quiet.

'The moment she touched the handle – which had always been slightly loose – it rattled and woke her.

One night, though, the door was left ajar and there was nothing to stop her passing through into the silent, carpeted corridor beyond' (page 1).

'They clattered across the back of the van, and Stella heard them thump down into the street, their footsteps fading' (page 67).

What does noise indicate? Does it indicate things being out in the open, whereas silence indicates secrecy? Are some places supposed to be noisy or quiet? A library for example. Why?

Think about which noises Stella hears from the back of the removal van, and when crouching in the cupboard and trying to escape in Chapter 34.

Discuss: When do you have quiet moments in your day? Is there ever silence? When is this? When is the noisiest part of your day?

Activity: Make a sound diary of your day. What are the first sounds you hear? Birds, an alarm clock, people? Can you separate the sounds into natural and artificial?

Make a sound map of your home: each room may have its own sound – the ticking of a clock, a radio normally on, a washing machine etc.

Can you write a dynamic description – pick a scene and try to describe what all the senses are experiencing. Try and base it on water – swimming or on a ferry for example.

Unsworth uses sound to suggest the magical realism elements of the sea:

'She could hear the steady pulse of the surf as it beat against the shore, and the long, muttering intake of its breath as it drew back again' (page 70.)

Discuss: How does Unsworth make the sea itself like a character?

'How strange the water felt against her skin. Now that she had become used to the cold, she was aware of another sensation, gentle, yet oddly urgent. She cocked her head, listening. It was like voices in a far-off room, she thought, or a swarm of insects half a field away. Something that you sensed was there, although you couldn't quite hear it. A feeling rather than a sound...' (page 71).

Discuss: How else could a writer make the ocean seem magical?

Activity: Write a paragraph about the ocean, giving it magic in some way. How have you done this? Which words did you use?

Stella's mum's necklace is 'the word of the sea', it turns out it keeps Stella safe in the water. Think about how else it helps Stella — it gives reassurance, gives her courage.

At the beginning of the book: 'She stood in the middle of the playground, and kids jostled and raced around her as if she was invisible' (page 12).

Discuss: Is Stella invisible by the end of the story? How does she make herself seen and heard by the end of the book?

In *The Little Mermaid* by Hans Christian Andersen, the mermaid sacrifices her voice so that she can gain legs and survive on land.

Discuss: How important is the voice? How can you make yourself heard without a voice? What else do we mean by 'having a voice'?

Characters

Stella

'It was as if she didn't notice — or see the need — of rows and borders, and separate places for things' (page 7), 'The mugs in the kitchen were made to line up...' (page 8), 'passing the identical houses with their neat front gardens and tidy driveways' (page 26).

Discuss: Stella is preoccupied with things being boring and orderly, and seeks change and disarray — like her mother. Why do you think this is?

Activity: Take a note of things you see on your way to school over several weeks. Are things neat and orderly, or is your local environment more higgledy-piggledy? Why do you think towns and houses are often arranged in some kind of order or grids?

Does your view change over time? Make a note of what changes take place over the weeks.

'"What a strange girl you are!"' Mrs Chapman says to Stella (page 4).

'"Do you think I'm strange, Gramma?" she asked one day.

Gramma smiled. "Isn't everyone?"' (page 23).

'"In my opinion, the more you know a person, the stranger they become"' (page 24).

'"You're not the same, same, same," she said. "You're weird"' (page 33).

'"You really *are* weird.'

"I know I am," Stella said. It was what she always said when Cam told her she was weird, which was quite often. It had become their private joke' (page 35).

'Cam had been right to laugh at her, she thought. Only a child of five would wonder whether her mum had been a mermaid or not. And even then, the child of five would have to be pretty stupid. The sort of child, Stella told herself, who caused people to shake their heads and whisper behind their hands' (page 58).

Stella is very concerned about what other people think, and is upset that Cam laughs at Stella for her beliefs.

'Her lovely mum had been a regular, normal human being. And Stella wasn't strange, or different in any way' (page 93).

'"It's not true," she whispered. "I can't change into anything. I'm normal"' (page 167).

'A hundred times wilder, and a hundred times more alien than any mermaid ever dreamed of' (page 191).

'Human. Normal. Pure relief welled up in her, and hand in hand with the relief, a quiet yet terrible sadness' (page 216).

Discuss: What do the characters mean by being 'strange' or 'weird'? What's the difference between 'weird-weird' and 'weird-*interesting*', as Cam says on page 33. What other words could Stella use to describe herself other than 'strange' or 'weird'? Are these derogatory words? Is she anomalous? What does it mean to be 'normal' or 'regular' or 'alien'? Why does Stella feel relief and sadness at the realisation that she is 'normal'?

Activity: Think about the things you believe in – write them down as a list. Write down examples of things you like or dislike. Now swap lists with a partner/classmate. Tick items on the list that you agree with. Do the differences mean that you are 'strange'? Think about ways in which you could celebrate the diversity around you – the different beliefs, customs, likes and dislikes.

Cam

'Cam liked to be dramatic and funny and *interesting*' (page 48).

'Cam exaggerated everything, Stella thought, you couldn't rely on a word she said' (page 54).

'"If me and that sofa were about to fall off a cliff, my mum would save the sofa," Cam had said. "It's the truth, swear on my life"' (page 61).

'Even asleep, Cam couldn't help being dramatic, Stella thought' (page 203).

Discuss: Why is the word 'interesting' italicised in the first quote? Think about how Cam uses exaggeration. When do you use exaggeration? Is it different for different purposes: To tell a story, to make a point, use persuasive language, to make an argument, for humorous effect?

Look at the different times Cam uses exaggeration, and when they are effective. See page 200 for when Cam 'exaggerates' their way onto the ferry. Is there a danger to exaggerating things? When does exaggeration become a lie?

Gramma

'The more she lost, the more the kindness showed, like a rock on the beach when the tide was going out' (page 52).

Stella wants to see pictures of her mother: 'It would make her mum feel real to Stella again, still alive, if only in memory' (page 98).

'Gramma was always right, Stella thought. One way or another' (page 162).

Discuss: Tania Unsworth makes Gramma a grounding influence in the story, despite her dementia. Why is this?

Is Gramma the only adult upon whom Stella can rely?

Activity: Stella finds out about her mother through her grandmother's memories of the past. Conduct an interview with an elderly member of your own family and see what memories they have of your parents or relatives that you might not be aware of. Share them in class. Has anyone found out anything surprising or different about their parents?

Dad

'"Grief or no grief, a dad ought to spend more time at home…"' (page 18).

'Stella hadn't thought about her dad during the long hours in the removal van. Yet underneath, she'd known that Mrs Chapman would have called him the instant she found Stella missing, and that he would have come home at once, upset, maybe even *frantic*' (page 78).

'*He doesn't always know the right thing to say,* you know, *Gramma had once told her. But he has a very good heart.*

Gramma never knew what she was talking about, Stella thought. Yet somehow, she was always, always right' (page 227–8).

Discuss: Do you think Stella's Dad is a good father? What makes a good father? Stella's father is one of the only men mentioned in the novel. Did you notice this? Why do you think the author has made all the characters female? If one was male – a grandfather instead of a grandmother, or Marcie being a man rather than a woman – would it have made a difference to the story? Think about the gender decisions an author must make in writing their novel.

Marcie and Pearl

Reread chapters 18 and 19.

Discuss: How does the author build tension to reveal that Marcie is the villain of the story? Pick out quotes as evidence. Look at the use of light and dark as well as the dialogue.

'Her skin lacked colour, and her hair was thin and wispy. Even her shabby dress, faded to a greenish memory, looked washed out. As if she had been painted entirely in watercolours' (page 97).

Discuss: What is Stella's first impression of Pearl? How does it change when she sees her up close? How has the author portrayed Pearl's weakness?

'At first glance, the stone looked like an ordinary pebble. But it was marbled with fine green veins, and when it caught the light in the right way, it gleamed with a dark fire, richer than velvet' (page 10).

Discuss: In what way is the stone like Pearl, or Stella's mother? What turns something ordinary into something special? Think about the first impressions in the book.

Activity: Can you write the scene in which Stella meets Pearl for the first time from Pearl's point of view? What emotions does she feel upon seeing

Aquabelle's daughter?

Discuss: Now look at chapters 27 to 31. Tania Unsworth switches point of view to Pearl telling her story. Why does she do this? Does the character of Marcie become more sinister as Pearl tells the story? How? Look at how Marcie sees Pearl and Aquabelle, and how she acts cruelly. Does this show Marcie's strength or Pearl's weakness? What are Marcie's boots a symbol of?

Themes

Mermaids

Stella's mum used to swim 'As if she was made of water itself' (page 3). Her hair 'glittered at the edges like a red-gold crown' (page 3) and 'shone like polished copper"' (page 10). She was 'too beautiful for this world' (page 22).

Compare this with the description of mermaids on page 21:

> 'According to legend, mermaids could bring on storms and tell the future, she read. Some were sirens, luring sailors to their doom; others had mysterious healing powers. All were beautiful, with flowing hair

and graceful features. They liked nothing better than to perch on rocks, admiring their reflections, or to glide through their underwater kingdoms, strewn with jewels and treasure—'

Discuss and Activity: Think about your stereotypical idea of a mermaid. Can you draw it? Why do mermaids hold such fascination for writers? How are mermaids viewed in different cultures? Do some research and present your findings in a PowerPoint. Compare ideas of mermaids as being inconsistent/vulnerable/protectors.

Now, look up the story of *The Little Mermaid* by Hans Christian Andersen. Why do you think it is so popular? Can you find a picture of the statue of *The Little Mermaid* in Copenhagen? How does this compare to the drawing you have done?

'"I used to think my mum was a mermaid…" she said. "Ages and ages ago," she added hastily. Cam shrugged. "I used to think my mum was a witch. And I still do"' (page 36).

'Away with the fairies, poor little thing, such a terrible shame' (page 58).

Discuss: How do ideas of mythical creatures come into our language and stories? Why do we have images of these creatures?

Activity: Mermaids are hybrids — half-human half-fish. Can you create your own mythical hybrid? What assets would it have, what kind of body and abilities?

Can you use your descriptive language to write about the underwater life of a mermaid? How would they live? What dangers might they encounter?

Using a shoebox, make an underwater diorama — think about which craft materials could represent water, and all the elements within. Will yours be deep ocean or a coral reef? Explore the possibilities.

Only when mermaids become nameless, do they take on non-stereotypical element:

'"There's no such thing, if you mean those creatures who sit on rocks and comb their hair all day," Pearl said, with a hint of scorn. "The ones with pretty tails, who sing to ships, or change into seals, or lure sailors to their doom with no apparent reason. There's no such thing as *them*."

"What, then?"

"Imagine what you would need to live in the deepest, wildest ocean," Pearl said. "The eel's whip and the limpet's cling, the strength and sleepless eyes of the great white shark, the liquid shiver of the squid... like *that*"' (page 123).

'"We're not called anything. We don't need language in the way you think of it. Names are no use to us. We are just... of the sea"' (page 137) Pearl explains to Stella.

'Now she knew that somewhere, deep below those waves, there were nameless beings, beyond the need for words or language. They had always been there, too swift to be caught, too cunning to be trapped, each cell in their bodies able to think, and feel, and understand' (page 203).

Discuss: If something is given a name or a label, is it too easy to attribute a stereotype to it? Think about common occupations, such as footballer, farmer or teacher. Does a stereotyped image come to mind? These stereotypes don't matter, and can be helpful, as long as they do not affect our attitude towards individuals.

Activity: Create a role play situation in small groups and examine stereotypes and prejudices. Invite a 'stereotype' to a party and see what people's reactions are. Then discuss whether these attitudes are prejudiced.

Body vs. Mind

There are many instances in the novel, in which it feels as if a person's body doesn't fit with their mind, and vice versa. Have a look at the following:

'As if her mind was so far away that her body had simply been left behind' (page 9).

'Stella's mum had had extremely large feet for her height. They looked, Stella often thought, as if they didn't quite belong to her' (page 24).

'Gramma looked different, taller, and yet somehow further away.' (page 55).

'She leaned over the railing and saw her own shadow, racing along on the surface of the water. Stella knew it was hers; it lifted an arm when she did, and she could see the tiny shape of her necklace dangling clear. But it looked different, thinner, almost sinuous. And the purposeful way it was moving was even more odd. As if it wasn't a shadow, but something separate and alive' (page 81–2).

'...her hair floating around her like a separate, living thing' (page 133).

Stella's mother seems separate from her body.

'On the screen, her mum's body glowed and shifted' (page 134).

'I didn't like the way I felt in my new skin. The flat thud of my feet, the dullness of my senses... Even worse I'd lost connection to most of my body. My heart was beating, blood ran through my veins and nerves fired my muscles, but I couldn't control any of it... It was like existing inside a machine' (page 141).

Discuss: How would it feel to have a mermaid body?

Activity: Look at how fish breathe underwater — make a poster to show the differences between human and fish respiration.

Friendship

'There were rules to making friends' (page 12).

Discuss: What does Stella mean by this?

Activity: Make a chart of friendship rules. Now look through the book. When do Stella and Cam adhere to your rules and when do they break them?

Stella and Cam's friendship is key to the story. Think about your own friendships.

Activity: Finish the following sentences as if you were Stella writing about Cam. Now do the same as yourself:

I like to have a friend because—
I make up with a friend by—
Having a friend makes me feel—

Memories

In the novel, the character of Gramma has dementia:

'Despite her efforts, her memories began to grow thin' (page 8).

'Her memories didn't follow each other in order; they were more like a well-shuffled deck of cards. There was no way of telling which would come out on top' (page 22).

'Her grandmother was a time traveller, Stella thought. She was always arriving — with great delight and surprise - into her own future' (page 28).

'Her dad looked at her thoughtfully. "I don't think your gramma has forgotten anything," he said. "I believe her memories are in there somewhere. She has trouble finding them when she needs to, that's all'" (page 226).

Discuss and Activity: What is dementia? Do you know anyone with dementia? Make a poster describing what dementia is.

Now do your own memory exercises. Take a tray with 10 small objects, such as a whistle, an acorn. Look at the tray for one minute, then cover it and see how many objects you can remember. Was it difficult/easy? Increase the number of objects. Which object is easiest to remember?

Play the shopping list game in a circle. Now think about why some things are more difficult to remember than others. How did you feel when you couldn't remember something? Was it frustrating?

Tania Unsworth uses 'memories' in other ways in the novel too. Look at the following quote:

'He used to be good at playing games but since her mum died, he had forgotten how to' (page 12–13).

Discuss: Has Stella's father really forgotten how to play? What does the author mean by this?

Pearl blames forgetfulness for them revealing that they are mermaids: 'I had to pinch Aquabelle to remind her where she was' (page 150).

Discuss: Had Aquabelle really forgotten where she was?

> 'In the memory, Stella was standing next to the window, and she must have been very young because her head only came up to the level of her mum's hands. She was showing her mum something in a book. It was a picture of a mermaid. Her mum looked down at the page.
>
> "There's no such thing," she said.
>
> Stella wasn't sure why she remembered this tiny incident, out of all the thousands of others. Maybe it had stuck in her mind because her mum's voice had sounded different. Not sharp — her mum was never sharp — but unusually abrupt. Or maybe it was the way Stella had felt in that moment. As if she had done something wrong without knowing quite what' (page 24–25).

'Stella thought they might have stayed dancing like that for ever, if they hadn't seen her standing there.

She gazed at Pearl, her mind bright with the memory' (page 122).

Discuss: Stella has lots of memories of her mother, and they evoke different emotions in her. Try and describe the emotions. Can you think of some early childhood memories? Do you think they are real or have you embellished them with things people have told you since? How can we tell a memory is real?

Activity: Write about an early childhood memory. Think carefully about the emotions you are trying to evoke.

© Clare Zinkin, Children's Reading Consultant